STORNOWAY

R17
Now
March '94

WESTERN ISLE

D1433215

Readers are requested to take great care of the books in their
possession, and to point out any defects that they may notice in them
to the Librarian.

This book is issued for a period of twenty-one days and should be
returned on or before the latest date stamped below, but an extension
of the period of loan may be granted when desired.

DATE OF RETURN	DATE OF RETURN	DATE OF RETURN
. . . .	. . . .	. . . .
. . . .	. . . .	. . . .
. . . .	. . . .	. . . .
. . . .	. . . .	. . . .
. . . .	. . . .	. . . .
. . . .	. . . .	. . . .
. . . .	. . . .	. . . .
. . . .	. . . .	. . . .
. . . .	. . . .	. . . .
. . . .	. . . .	. . . .
. . . .	. . . .	. . . .
. . . .	. . . .	. . . .
. . . .	. . . .	. . . .
. . . .	. . . .	. . . .

HEINEMANN
NEW WINDMILLS

THE NOT-JUST-ANYBODY FAMILY

When he hears the cry "Police!" Vern has only one reaction—run! Vern thinks running from the police is the only intelligent thing for a Blossom to do. The police might have been put on earth to help some people, but never a Blossom!

But when Vern and Maggie stop running they're not sure what to do next. They left Junior with wings attached about to fly off the barn and by the time they get home he has completely vanished. What's more, their grandfather hasn't come home yet.

Then Vern hits on a plan—a plan to find their grandfather and to find out exactly what is going on . . .

ABOUT THE AUTHOR

Betsy Byars was born in North Carolina, the daughter of a cotton mill worker. Although she read a great deal as a child, she didn't want to be a writer but rather to work with animals. Later on, married and the mother of four young children, she began to write articles for newspapers and magazines. She began to write stories for children as her own children were growing up.

In 1970 she won the Newberry medal for The Summer of the Swans and in that year The Midnight Fox was her first book to be published in Great Britain. She has written over twenty books for children.

Betsy Byars now lives with her husband in South Carolina. She is a licensed pilot and spends a considerable amount of her time travelling in pursuit of her interest in gliding and antique aircraft.

THE
Not-Just-Anybody Family

BETSY BYARS

HEINEMANN
NEW WINDMILLS

Heinemann Educational
a division of
Heinemann Educational Books Ltd
Halley Court, Jordan Hill, Oxford OX2 8EJ
OXFORD   LONDON   EDINBURGH
MADRID   PARIS   ATHENS   BOLOGNA
MELBOURNE   SYDNEY   AUCKLAND
IBADAN   NAIROBI   GABORONE   HARARE
SINGAPORE   TOKYO   PORTSMOUTH (NH)   KINGSTON

First published by The Bodley Head 1986
First published in the New Windmill Series 1992

93 94 95 10 9 8 7 6 5 4 3 2

British Library Cataloguing in Publication Data
for this title is available from the British Library

ISBN 0 435 12384 X

Cover illustration by Julie Dodd

Typeset by Cambridge Composing (UK) Ltd
Printed and bound in England by Clays Ltd, St Ives plc

For Eddie

On and off the Barn

Junior stood on top of the barn, arms out-stretched, legs apart. Strapped to his thin arms were wings made out of wire, old sheets, and staples—his own design. His mouth hung open. His eyes watched a spot over the cornfield where he hoped to land. He appeared to be praying.

"Go ahead and jump," his brother, Vern, called.

"Give him time," his sister, Maggie, said. She was sitting cross-legged on the ground, painting her finger-nails with a green Magic Marker.

"Well, if he doesn't jump before Pap gets home, he won't get to jump. Junior, Pap won't let you jump. If he catches you up there on the barn, he'll whup you."

Junior kept watching the small grassy clearing beyond the cornfield. He was trying to watch it long enough to make it his body's destination. He felt his body had to know where it was supposed to go or it would end up twenty feet straight down in the hard dirt.

"Are you going to fly or not?" Vern asked.

Maggie held up one hand to admire her green fingernails and to blow on them, although they were dry. When she got the other hand done, she was going to make herself some rings out of

7

clover. She loved to have beautiful hands because you could admire them so easily.

She showed her hand to Vern. "What do you think?"

"Are you going to fly or not?" Vern asked again.

Junior did not answer. His body was getting ready. He could actually feel strength seeping into his arms. The wings were actually becoming part of him, like a bird's.

This was the third time Junior had climbed up on the barn and allowed Vern to tie on his wings, the third time he had inched his way out to the edge of the roof. But this was the first time he had felt his body actually getting ready to participate, the first time strength had flowed into his arms.

His tongue flicked over his dry lips.

"He's not going," Vern said. His voice was heavy with scorn. "He just wants us to stand out here and beg him."

Maggie said, "Give him time."

"That's what we been doing. Every afternoon we been giving him . . ."

He trailed off because he knew from past experience that it was impossible to predict what Junior would actually do. Junior was going to be a stunt man when he grew up, and sometimes he did things to prove he could, like going down Red Hill on a car made of an apple crate and two skates. "Good-bye, Red Hill," Junior had called, letting go with one hand to wave. Other times, like the day he had pretended he was going over White Run Falls with an inflated garbage bag under each arm—that had come to nothing.

Since there was no way of being sure, Vern waited. In his boredom he tried to blow a bubble with his gum, but his gum was five days old. Vern was going to chew it for a solid week. Since the second day it had been like chewing a rubber band. The only way he could have any fun with it now was to pull it out and twist it around his tongue. He did this without taking his eyes off Junior.

"Junior, you going or not?" he called.

Junior kept watching the grassy patch between the cornfield and the road.

Maggie finished her other hand, but it wasn't as nice as the first one. She had gone out of the nails in three places. "I couldn't stand to be left-handed, could you?" she asked Vern.

Vern put his gum back into his mouth. He was standing on one leg now, like a flamingo, with the other foot braced on his knee.

Junior took a deep breath, filling his lungs with warm country air—it couldn't hurt to have your lungs inflated with air when you jumped. The thought of his lungs as balloons was comforting to him. Maybe he wouldn't even need the wings. Maybe he would just float. What a surprise that would be. Vern and Maggie—

Vern saw the expression on Junior's face. "He's going." He spoke in the muted voice he used on the rare occasions when he got to the movies and didn't want to disturb the people around him. He'd sit there, gripping the armrests, telling himself what was going to happen:"He's going to crash. . . . He's going to get his head blown off," until he did disturb somebody and they said, "Will you shut up!"

Maggie looked up from her nails. The top of the Magic Marker was in her mouth, so her mouth looked like a small green circle. She removed it. "Don't hurt yourself, Junior," she called.

Junior nodded without taking his eyes from the grassy clearing. He now thought of the clearing as his destination, the way a pilot thinks of an airport. He could see the very spot—that deep patch of clover—where he would touch down.

Vern knew that just before Junior flew, he would call "Good-bye, Barn." Everyone in the family had tried to break Junior of the habit of saying good-bye to houses and trees and barns, but no one had succeeded.

"It's stupid," Vern had told him. "They can't hear you."

"Maybe, maybe not," Junior had answered, closing his eyes in an expression that made him look, he thought, wise.

Junior exhaled and took another of his deep inflating breaths. Then he paused. Something beyond the clearing had caught his attention.

A small cloud of dust was moving on the road. Junior watched it first with irritation. Pap was coming home early.

Every Monday afternoon Pap went into town with a truckload of beer and pop cans, which they collected from Highway 123 and petrol station rubbish bins and picnic areas. Today Pap must have sold them fast and was already coming home.

Junior knew he would have to fly right this minute or wait till tomorrow. And he didn't want to do either. He felt he was almost ready—maybe another ten minutes and he would actually fly.

Frown lines came between his eyebrows as he squinted into the distance. He attempted to bring one hand up to shield his eyes so he could see better. He had forgotten this was not possible while you were wearing wings. It was also not possible to wipe the sweat off your chin or scratch where you itched.

He leaned forward slightly.

Seeing the forward motion, mistaking it for a step off the roof, Vern cried, "He's going!"

Junior stopped at the edge of the roof. He saw now that it was not Pap's truck. Pap's truck would be raising more dust. Pap's truck rattled louder than that. Pap's truck didn't have a shiny new bumper. Pap's truck didn't have a blue light on top.

He took one step backward. His wings dragged on the worn roof. He could see what it was now. He gasped with fear. "It's—it's—"

"What's wrong this time?" Vern said. "What's your big excuse this time? Coward! Yellow-belly! Either you jump or I'm going in the house, and

11

I'm not kidding. And I'm not coming back either. I knew you weren't going to fly. You're nothing but a lousy yellow-bellied coward!"

"It's—it's—"

Junior raised one white wing to point to the dusty road. His eyes looked over their heads. He had stopped breathing. He was like a statue pointing. *The Winged Sentinel.*

And then he said one of the most dreaded words in the family vocabulary.

"Police!"

Running Scared

"Police!" Junior screamed again.

"Police?" Maggie said.

She got to her feet like a startled deer. She heard in the distance the hum of an unfamiliar engine, an engine perfectly maintained, ready to give chase. "It *is* the police."

"Let's get out of here," Vern said. As he started to run he shouted, "Hide, Junior!"

Maggie flicked her braids over her shoulders and followed. She and Vern ran for their lives, around the barn, past the house, down the gully where Pap threw the household trash. Stumbling over rusty fenders, old bottles, rotten wood, papers, they headed for the woods.

"Wait!"

They barely heard Junior's desperate cry. They ducked through the trees. They knew these woods because they had been running through them all their lives, running from each other mostly, but now it was as if all that had been practice for this moment.

Without a word they dodged through the trees. At the creek they skidded down the bank and jumped together. They kept running.

Not until they were three miles into the woods,

past the ravine, did they stop. Then, by mutual unspoken consent—they both knew they were too far into the woods for the police to follow— they flung themselves down on the soft green moss.

Vern had landed on his back and was lying with his eyes shut, mouth open, hands crossed over his chest. He was breathing so hard and fast, his throat stung.

Maggie was wincing, holding her side because every time she ran fast, it hurt. Her green-tipped fingers pressed hard into the flesh beneath her jeans.

Maggie played different solitary games in different parts of the thick, untouched forest. Here, in this pine-ringed clearing, was where she usually played Hiawatha, but Indian games were not on her mind today.

She was the first one to get her breath. "What do you think?"

Vern couldn't speak yet. He shook his head without opening his eyes.

"What do you think they wanted?" Maggie asked.

Again Vern shook his head.

"Maybe it wasn't the police," Maggie said. "Did you ever think of that?"

"It was the police," Vern managed to say.

"We didn't see them. I didn't. All I heard was Junior yelling 'Police!' Maybe he did that to keep from flying. Maybe it was just—oh, some person who'd turned into our road by mistake."

14

"Junior wouldn't lie about something like that. It sure sounded like a police car."

High in a tree a woodpecker worked on an old branch.

Maggie kept thinking. She was trying to come up with some optimistic reason for the arrival of the police. She couldn't. Finally she said, "Maybe Pap was in an accident."

Again Vern shook his head, this time because he didn't think that was what had happened.

"Maybe dead."

Another head shake.

"Then what?" she asked impatiently.

Vern lifted his shoulders and let them fall. Slowly with great effort, he sat up.

Suddenly he was aware that his chewing gum—his constant companion for five days—was missing. He didn't know if he had swallowed it or if it had popped out while he was running. He opened his eyes.

Maggie's side felt better, so she lay down beside him. She crossed her braids over her chest. Squinting up at the bright July sky, she asked again, "What do you think?"

Vern's mind had started working. This time he shook his head because he was thinking and didn't want to be disturbed.

When he had first heard the cry "Police!" from the top of the barn, he had had only one reaction, an instant reaction—run.

He had not questioned it or thought about it. It was the exact same reaction his grandfather

15

would have had. Running from the police was the only intelligent thing for a Blossom to do. The police might have been put on earth to help some people, but never a Blossom.

"I think that they were looking for Pap to arrest him," Vern said finally.

"Why? What do you think he did? Could it be because his licence plate's no good?"

"They don't arrest you for that. They give you tickets."

"Maybe they know that Pap's been making booze in the basement."

"Maybe."

"What are we going to do, Vern?"

Vern scratched his head. When he was six years old, he blew off half of one finger. He had found a dynamite cap, an interesting black cylinder, and, not knowing what it was, had tried to break it open to see what was inside.

He took a sort of pride in his finger, and was glad when some kid asked him what had happened to it. His happiest moment in school had come on the first day of second grade.

The teacher had explained second grade and all the interesting things they would be doing, and then she had said, "Any questions, boys and girls?"

The boy next to Vern raised his hand.

"Yes?" the teacher asked.

"My question is, What happened to that boy's finger?"

"Dynamite," Vern answered.

"What are we going to *do*?" Maggie asked again. She knew that when Vern scratched his head with his dynamited finger, he was thinking hard.

"I'm not through thinking," he said.

Junior's Miss

"Wait!"

From his desperate perch atop the barn Junior watched them go.

"Wait for me! You guys wait for me!" he cried. "Wait!"

His brother and sister disappeared into the trees, and Junior's heart sank like a stone.

His heart felt so low, he wanted to put his hand on his chest and make sure it had not actually dropped into his stomach, that it was still in his chest where it was supposed to be. He would have done this if it had not been for the wings.

The police car was out of sight now, driving through the stretch of pine trees by the creek. Junior heard the rattle of boards as the car drove slowly over the old board bridge.

Black crows called a warning and flew out of the trees towards the barn. They glided so close, Junior could hear the rush of their wings.

Suddenly, in a panic, Junior swirled and dived for the door to the loft. His wings stopped him at the sill. He fell back with a cry of frustration and fear.

He began tearing at his wings, trying to grab

them through the cloth that covered his hands. It was as if the wings were actually part of his body. They wouldn't move.

The strings! He got one in his teeth and pulled so hard, he got the first loose tooth of his life, something he had been waiting for for years. He did not notice.

His brother, Vern, had tied all the knots and spat on them. "Now," Vern had said, "there's no way those are coming loose." Vern knew what he was talking about.

"Get off my arms!" Junior begged the wings. He was beginning to cry now. "Get off!"

He was more desperate than he had been the time the hornets got after him, only he had been able to outrun them. He was fast enough to outrun anything in the whole world, but he couldn't do a thing with these horrible wings on his arms. They were like traps.

And, he went on, tears filling his eyes, he would rather have hornets after him any day in the week than the police.

"Get *off*!"

The police car was coming around the curve now, pulling into the clearing by the barn. Junior could see it, and he dropped to his knees. He crouched against the side of the barn, hiding behind the wings.

The car passed the barn and stopped in front of the house. Junior could hear the doors slam as the police got out of the car.

Tears were running down his cheeks. He was

choking silently on his sobs. He was so full of tears, he thought he was going to drown. It was worse than the time he almost did drown down at the creek, trying to stay underwater longer than Vern.

"Anybody home?" one policeman called. He tried to ring the door bell, but it had not worked in ten years. He rattled the screen door.

"Don't let them see me," Junior pleaded. His head was buried in his wings. "Please don't let them see me. I'll be good for the rest of my life if you just don't let them see me. I'll give you a hundred million dollars if you don't let them see me."

"I'll check around the back," one policeman said.

"I'll check the barn."

Barn! As soon as the word was spoken Junior's wings began to flutter.

"Nobody back here," the policeman called as he rounded the house. His voice was comfortingly far away.

Then, from inside the barn, right below Junior's trembling wings, the policeman called, "Nobody in here either."

Junior could hear the policeman walking around, kicking old straw as if he hoped to find somebody hiding underneath. Junior felt he knew the exact second the policeman looked up at the loft, deciding whether to climb the ladder.

Junior held his breath. Then the policeman

20

walked out and stood exactly where Vern had stood, waiting for Junior's flight.

"Well, what do you think? Think we ought to wait?"

The other policeman joined him, standing in Maggie's place. Across the yard the patrol car's radio sputtered with sound, and Junior pleaded silently, *Somebody's calling you! Go answer!*

The policemen stayed where they were, by the barn, one in Maggie's place, one in Vern's.

And, Junior thought with another anxious flutter of his wings, the reason Maggie and Vern had picked that spot was because it was where they had the best view of him on the roof.

"We can come back later."

"Right."

Still they stood there. Why didn't they go? Junior wanted to peer around his wings, but he was not going to do that until they were a million miles away. No, a billion miles away. If he just stayed absolutely still . . .

"What's that up there on the roof?"

Junior's heart stopped beating.

"Where?"

"Up there."

Maybe they meant the house roof, Junior thought, his wings trembling so hard, it was as if they were real. His thoughts bounded frantically in his brain. Please let them mean the house roof. Please—

"Up there."

"On the barn?"

"Yes."

"Is it some kind of kite? What is that thing?"

"That's what I was asking you."

At that moment, the worst moment of his life, Junior felt himself begin to slide. He tried to catch himself. He gave one frantic lurch, but somehow this left him doubled over, his wings pinned beneath him.

He picked up speed. He might as well have been on a sledge. He began a long, high-pitched scream. He was sliding face down, and somehow this made it even scarier.

Another frantic lunge flipped him over, and he looked up into the blinding July sun. He was now on the very spot where he had stood with such hope only moments before.

He was at the edge of the roof, his legs dangling in space. He tottered there, as if on a see-saw, and then he went over.

As he fell his arms rose from his sides, and he began desperately to beat the air with them. He had a brief, startlingly clear picture of himself taking flight, soaring over the policemen's heads to the grassy clearing and then beyond, actually skimming the sky like a bird.

Good-bye, World.

The beautiful vision ended as he hit the hard ground at the feet of the startled policemen.

Broken Wings

Vern and Maggie were creeping up on the house in the darkness. They were on their stomachs, edging forward on their elbows like soldiers.

The only sounds were the chirping of the crickets and tree frogs and the occasional whine of a hungry mosquito.

They paused in the shadows. Ahead of them the moonlight turned the clearing white.

"Well, their car's gone," Maggie said.

"Maybe it's parked in a different place."

"There are no lights on in the house," she said, trying to make things better. "Wouldn't they put lights on if they were inside?"

"Not if they were trying to catch us off guard."

"Oh."

This exchange and Maggie's soft "Oh" gave Vern a feeling of manliness, of being in charge. He felt he alone understood the wiles of the policemen, the tricks they played on the innocent. It was going to be up to him to save them all.

He paused to give their secret whistle, to alert Junior they were in the yard. *Bobwhite! Bobwhite!* The whistle hung on the air like the actual song of a bird.

They waited.

There was no answering call from Junior.

"Stay here," Vern said.

In a crouch he ran through the moonlit clearing and into the bushes around the house. These bushes were as old as the house—seventy years old; and they were so overgrown, a four-door car could disappear in their branches.

Vern ran around to the front of the house behind the bushes. He went up the steps silently, taking them one by one. From the top step he slipped across the porch.

The porch swing had been raised last fall. Pap stored it by pulling it up to the ceiling so it couldn't bang against the house during winter storms. This spring he had not got around to letting it down.

Vern paused under the swing, listening.

Then he lifted his head and peered into the room. Everything was still.

He duck-walked to the door and paused at the screen door. Nothing looked out of order. The house smelt the way it always did. At this point he almost felt he could, like his grandfather and his grandfather's dog, Mud, smell a stranger if one was inside.

In a soft voice he said, "Junior?"

There was no answer.

Vern opened the door and went inside.

Like a shadow he moved through the rooms. "Junior," he said softly in each one. Junior might have hidden himself in a closet or under a bed.

It was too dark to see, but Vern knew every stick of furniture in every room. He could have gone through this house blindfold. In his lifetime not one single piece of furniture had been bought, nothing had been recovered, nothing had been painted, no new curtains had been hung. He felt the comfort of the familiar, almost—it seemed— friendly sofas and beds and chairs.

He opened the basement door. "Junior?" There was the familiar smell of warm fermenting mash, but no Junior.

At the back of the house Maggie waited with her chin resting on her hands. A mosquito, whining, landed on her cheek. She slapped it away.

It was too dark to see her green Magic Marker nails, but if she could have, it would not have brought her one bit of pleasure. She was going to scrub the green off as soon as she could get to the kitchen sink. Green nails were stupid and childish, and she somehow felt she had matured enormously just in the space of that afternoon.

Vern came through the darkness so silently that she gasped out loud when he dropped down beside her.

"I think they've gone."

"But where's Junior?"

"I don't know. He's not in the house."

"Do you think they caught Junior?"

The way she choked on the word *caught* made it sound like the worst thing that could happen to a person.

"Let's check the barn. Maybe he got inside and hid in the straw. That's what he should have done—that's what I meant for him to do when I yelled 'Hide!'" He added with a sigh, "Only, you know Junior."

"Yes."

"And keep quiet."

"All I said was 'Yes.'"

"Well, don't say it so loud. Those policemen could be anywhere."

"Anyway, I don't think he could hide with those wings on his arms," Maggie whispered.

Since this was the exact thing Vern was thinking, he said, "I asked you to be quiet."

In silence they crossed the yard to the barn, running through the moonlit clearing. They slipped behind the old sagging door.

This door hadn't been closed in five years. Even when their mom was home from the rodeo with her horse, Sandy Boy, they didn't close the door. The patch of weeds that grew behind the door was stiff and thorny and reached to their waists.

"Ow," said Maggie.

Vern looked at her in disgust, and she said, "Well, I stuck myself on a thorn." She put her knuckle into her mouth to ease the pain.

Vern peered out around the barn door. "Come on, let's go in."

They slipped around the barn door and stopped short.

"Oh, Vernon," Maggie said, using his full name for the first time in years.

She reached for his hand. He reached for hers, but they were so upset, they did not touch. Their hands grabbed the air.

For in the moonlight, just beneath the spot where Junior had stood poised for flight, lay two broken, twisted, ruined objects, the saddest objects either Maggie or Vern had ever seen.

"Wings," they said together.

2,147 Beer and Pop Cans

Pap was in the corner cell of the city gaol. It was one o'clock in the morning, but Pap was not sleeping. He was sitting on his bunk, leaning over his knees, staring at nothing.

His brows were pulled low over his dark eyes. The blood was pumping so hard in his head, the blue veins were throbbing.

Pap was seventy-two years old, and this was the first time he had been arrested. It had been so upsetting that at first he had had to hold himself back from jumping up and actually trying to tear the bars off his cell. If he had been a younger man, at the peak of his strength, that is exactly what he would have done.

Now he sat without moving, except for the veins pumping in his head, and his elbows, which trembled against his legs. He had been sitting like this for five hours.

The arrest had happened so fast, it still bewildered him to think about it.

He had been coming up Sumter Avenue, minding his own business, stopping for stop signs, red lights, and pedestrians. He had to do this because he had an expired licence plate, and he did not want to call attention to himself.

He also had 2,147 beer and pop cans in the back of his truck in see-through plastic bags. This was the biggest haul Pap had ever made—the result of a July Fourth weekend bonanza.

It was such a mountain of cans that it caused heads to turn all up and down Sumter Avenue. Pap was proud of it. He got five cents for every can he brought in, and so in the back of his truck was $107.35 cold cash. He had multiplied it out on a brown paper bag. He couldn't wait to get to the station and reap his rewards.

Beside him on the seat was his dog, Mud. Mud was also enjoying the ride. He was looking out of the window, doing what Pap called smiling.

Mud had been Pap's dog for ten years, and when Pap was feeling good, Mud felt good. When Pap was low, Mud crawled under the porch and would not come out even if somebody called "Supper!"

Pap turned the corner and started up the steepest part of Spring Street. He was whistling.

Suddenly the car in front of him unexpectedly stopped to back into a parking space. Pap didn't crash into the back of the car, as he felt he certainly had a right to do, but he had to brake so hard that the back of the pick-up truck flopped down.

Pap heard a soft, rustling thud as the first bag of beer and pop cans tumbled onto Spring Street. It was a slow-motion kind of thing; the bag just toppled slowly onto the street. Then there was a second thud, and a third.

Pap cursed and pulled up his handbrake, and the old Chevrolet truck shuddered and died. Pap got out to see the damage.

He stood in the middle of the street, hands braced on the small of his back. He looked at the sorry spectacle of his bags of cans lying on the street. He was wagging his head back and forth.

At that moment two teenage boys in a Toyota cut around the corner. Pap turned with a frown. The boys ran into the bags like kids hitting a leaf pile. It looked to Pap as if they had done it on purpose.

The boys were laughing. The driver threw the Toyota into reverse, U-turned, and took off.

Pap reached into the back of his truck for his shotgun. He fired one shot at the retreating Toyota, but he hit the traffic light down the street. It exploded and left some wires sizzled and popping over the Sumter Avenue inter-section.

Two of the bags were busted, and Pap was standing over them, worrying about his $107.35, when he saw some people on the sidewalk. He turned to the people with a frown. He was thinking about asking for some help, even though asking for help was hard for him.

The people, however, thought he was pointing the shotgun at them. They divided. Half of them ran into the nearby Woolco, the other half into Winn Dixie.

The stupid fools! Couldn't they see it was a single-barrel shotgun? All he had wanted was some help, and he didn't even want that now; wouldn't let them help if they asked. Stupid fools!

He was trying to gather up the cans and get them back into the truck by himself when the police arrived—two carloads, sirens screaming.

"What's happened?" Pap wondered aloud. He thought maybe there was a bank robbery up the street.

But the police, guns out of their holsters, were advancing on him!

"Wait," he said. He took two steps backwards. "I ain't done nothing. I just want to get my cans and get out of here. I just—"

They never let him finish. Two of the policemen grabbed him and shoved him face down onto the bags of cans. Pap tried to get up.

The policemen were doing something to his arms. Pap didn't want them to. Suddenly Pap felt the bags break, and he heard cans rolling.

"My cans!" Pap cried. He was struggling in the cans now, sending them on their way faster.

The policemen got him to his feet, took his shotgun, handcuffed him, and threw him into the back of a police car. At one time it would have taken the entire police force to do this, but that was before Pap became seventy-two years old.

They started the police car and drove away while the people were coming out of Woolco and Winn Dixie. One by one the people lined up to tell the policeman with the notepad about Pap threatening them.

31

All this time the 2,147 pop and beer cans were rolling down Spring Street, across the Sumter intersection, and through the municipal parking lot. From there they rolled into White Run Creek. They were clicking like wood chimes.

In White Run Creek they started downstream, bobbing with the currents, turning the creek silver where the sun hit them.

See-Through Eyelids

It was Tuesday morning. Junior was dreaming, as he always did just before he woke up, that he could see through his eyelids.

This dream had become so real to Junior that he believed he could actually do it. Without opening his eyes, he could see his room and his window and the tree outside the window and the beautiful picture of his mother on Sandy Boy. In the picture his mother was leaning off the back of the horse, upside down, one foot in a strap behind the saddle. Sometimes Junior turned the picture around so he could see his mother right side up.

One time, in first grade, the teacher had said, "Now, boys and girls, I want you all to close your eyes because I want you to imagine something."

Dutifully Junior had closed his eyes and he had, through his eyelids—he was willing to swear this on a stack of bibles—through his eyelids he had seen Mrs Hodges adjust her brassiere.

This morning he knew, without opening the first eye, that he was somewhere he did not want to be. Beneath him the sheets were stiff and clean. There was a funny smell in the air. There was too much light. Somewhere outside the room a lot of people were doing things. Wheels were rolling. Ladies and men talking. A dread fell over him like a cover.

He opened his eyes and gasped with fear. It was the first time in his life he had awakened and not known where he was. He was either in a hospital or a prison, maybe a prison hospital. He had watched enough television to figure that out.

"I got to get out of here," he muttered.

He tried to sling his legs over the side of the bed, but they wouldn't go. It was as if his legs were actually attached to the foot of the bed. He sat up, threw back the sheet.

His legs were in white stiff things. They wouldn't budge. It was yesterday all over again, only now it was his legs that wouldn't work instead of his winged arms.

He began to cry. Under the white still things, where he couldn't get at them, his legs hurt. They hurt a lot. Just trying to sling them over the side of the bed had made pain shoot through his whole body.

"What's wrong?"

Junior couldn't have been more startled if God had spoken to him. He had not even been aware that anyone else was in the room. He glanced around so fast, his neck popped.

A redheaded boy in the next bed was watching him with interest.

"I don't know," Junior gasped.

"You must have been in an accident."

34

—

All the horror came back to him then. "I fell off a barrrrrrn," he wailed. He flung himself back against his pillow.

"A barn?"

Junior twisted his head from side to side, too miserable now to speak.

"What were you doing on a barn? Making like a rooster? *Er-er-errrrrrrrr-err!*" The boy flapped his arms at his sides.

Junior nodded, dumb with misery and pain.

"You were playing rooster? No kidding? You could go on *That's Incredible.*"

"I wasn't playing rooster. I was trying to fly."

"Did you?"

"Not farrrrr."

"How far? Ten feet? Twenty?"

The distance was so short, Junior could measure it with his hands. He showed the boy a distance of about three feet, then he let his hands drop to his sides.

He wiped his tears on his bed sheet. "Where are we?" he asked the boy.

"Alderson General Hospital, fourth floor."

Junior looked at the boy with grudging admiration. Here was someone who obviously knew a thing or two about hospitals.

"How did I get here?"

"They brought you down from the operating room last night, eleven o'clock. It woke me. You were moaning. *Oh, no, no, noooooooooooo.* Like that. The nurse said you broke both your legs, but she didn't say how."

"The barn."

Pity crept into Junior's voice. He wondered if he would ever again be able to say the word *barn* without wanting to weep.

"Don't you remember anything?"

Junior shook his head.

"They must have knocked you out. Or did they just go ahead and set your legs while you were awake?"

"I don't remember."

"Well, you'd remember if they'd knocked you out. You know how they do it? The doctor takes a great big hammer and he hides it behind his back and then he says, 'Look over there! Quick! What's that?' And when you look, he brings out the hammer and hits you over the head."

"That's not true," Junior said.

"Yes, it is. You know what they did to me?"

"No."

"They cut my head open and filled it with marbles. You can hear them rolling around when I shake my head."

"That's not true."

"Prove it," the boy said.

Junior was too busy going over his own memories to worry about the boy's marbles. To himself he said, *I was up on the barn and the police drove in the yard—I remember that, and I was hiding from them on the roof—I remember that, and I slipped.*

To the boy he added, "If I had been able to go off the roof the way I'd planned, sort of launch

36

myself, I could have escaped over the trees, but they got me all mixed up." Again sorrow made his voice quiver. "It was the police that made me fall."

"You probably wouldn't have flown anyway. People have not had a lot of luck with home-made wings. I saw a whole show that was nothing but people trying to fly—one man had a bicycle with wings on it and he pedalled it right off a cliff. Another man went off a bridge. You were probably lucky just to break two legs."

"That's all I've got." More pity.

"You've got other bones, though—hip-bones, jaw-bones, backbones."

It reminded Junior of a song they sang in the first grade: *"Dem bones, dem bones, dem dryyyyy bones."* He never had liked that song.

"You know what they do to you if you break your jaw-bone, don't you?"

"No."

"Wire your mouth shut so you can't eat for a month."

"That's not—"

A trolley rolled by the door. Junior, startled, broke off his sentence to swing his head around. "What was that?"

"When they take you to surgery, they put you on one of those trolleys."

"I'm not getting on a trolley," Junior said instantly. "No matter what happens, no matter what they say, I'm not getting on any trolley."

"If you won't get on the trolley, then they bring

the hammer in the room and hit you over the head right here. They did it to that boy that was in that bed right over there. I saw them. They had to hit him twice. One time he put his hand up to protect his head, and they hit him on the hand. He took his hand down, and they hit him on the head so hard, his eyes popped out."

"That's not t—"

Again Junior didn't get to finish what he was saying, because the nurse came in. He seemed to get smaller as he realised she was coming to his bed.

"Good morning."

The nurse handed Junior a tiny paper cup. He muttered "Thank you" before he saw there was a pink pill in it. Junior looked at it with suspicion.

"What's that?"

"It's your medicine," the nurse said.

Junior let the pill roll around in the cup. Sometimes Maggie played nurse with him, but she used ketchup for medicine.

"Now, open wide," Maggie would say. She'd pour some ketchup into a tablespoon, hold his nose, and poke the ketchup in.

He loved to play patient, but he didn't want to be one. Suddenly he was homesick. Maggie made a better nurse than anybody in this whole hospital. Tears filled his eyes.

The boy in the next bed said, "If you don't take your pill, they bring in a great big needle—thaaat long, and they give you a shot in your rear end."

38

"Now, Ralphie," the nurse warned, "you shouldn't scare Junior. He hasn't even been here one—"

Before she could finish, Junior had swallowed his pink pill. "Water?" He shook his head.

He handed the nurse the empty cup, lay back, and closed his eyes. For the first time in his life he was glad not to have see-through eyelids.

Going to Town

"I'm tired," Maggie said.

Vern said, "Keep walking."

"I can't. My flip-flop's broken."

"Fix it."

"Well, stop and give me a chance."

Without turning around, Vern stopped. He put his hands in his pockets. He sighed with impatience. He stared ahead at the road. Beyond the curve and the pointed pine trees a huge red sun was sinking. Vern was not admiring the view. He sighed again, louder. "We have a long way to go. We haven't even crossed the Interstate yet."

Maggie sat on the side of the road and pushed the worn piece of plastic back into the sole of her flip-flop. Then she slipped her dirty foot through the thong. Without getting up, she said, "I think we ought to call Mom."

"No."

"Why not?"

"I told you. We are only supposed to call if it's an emergency. You know that. The last thing Mom said was for us not to be calling all the time."

"This is an emergency."

"An emergency is what we can't handle ourselves."

"That's what this is. We can't handle this. Pap may be in gaol."

"We can handle it."

Vern did not turn around during this conversation. He just faced the sunset. His mouth was a straight line in his tired face.

The reason Vern spoke with such firmness about not calling their mom was that the week before, he had tried to call her himself. He had wanted to hear her voice so much that he had walked three miles to the Exxon station and stepped into the pay phone booth.

Every week their mom wrote postcards to let them know where she would be staying. Their mom still went on the rodeo circuit in the summers—she was a trick rider; and she never knew exactly what motel she would be staying at till she got there.

In Vern's hand was the latest postcard, the latest phone number.

When their dad was alive, they all went on the circuit. They had had a camper, and all three kids had slept on a table that made into a bed. Their parents slept over the cab.

Vern, who was old enough to remember those days, thought they were the happiest of his life. Just one long stretch of dusty, interesting days and bright nights. Even the rainy days and the mud had been fun.

Vern had looked again at the number. His

mom was staying this week at the Paisano Motel. There was a picture of a long brick motel with a sign shaped like a sombrero. The number was printed in big letters. He dialled them.

"Is this a credit card call?" the operator asked.

"No, I've got money," he said. The money was lined up on the shelf under the phone—quarters, then dimes, then nickels, neat as a bank.

"Deposit three dollars and thirty cents."

It took Vern a long time to get that much money into the phone, but it was worth it. Immediately the phone began to ring and a voice said, "Paisano Motel."

Vern cleared his throat. "Could I speak with Vicki Blossom?"

"Who?"

"Vicki Blossom. She's staying there."

"She's not registered."

"She has to be."

"Nope. No Blossom."

"She's with the rodeo."

"Honey, everybody staying at this motel is with the rodeo."

"But this is my mom. She gave me this number."

He was horrified to hear his voice break on the word *mom*. Now the hotel manager would think he was a child. If his mom did come, she would say, "Your little boy called. He sounded like he was crying."

In a mature, adult voice he said, "Well, if she

42

does check in, would you tell her Vern called, and everything is all right here."

"I will, hon."

"Thank you."

"You're welcome."

He stood, hands in his pockets, staring down the highway. The shadows were getting longer. The traffic was getting sparse. Everybody was either home for supper or going home for supper but them.

Maggie got to her feet. "I still think we ought to call."

Vern swirled around. Remembering the incomplete phone call made his eyes even harder. "I told you I can handle it!"

"Well, I'm the oldest and I ought to be the one to decide when we handle it and when we don't."

"Look, you want to call—go ahead. Be my guest. Call."

At that moment he looked so much older than Maggie that the eleven months that separated them might as well have been eleven years. He stared at her with eyes that did not blink once.

Maggie blinked seven or eight times. She said, "Vern, I can't call. I don't have any monnnnnnney."

He turned and started walking. To Maggie it was the way John Wayne walked into the sunset when he wasn't coming back. Quickly she got to her feet.

"Wait for meeeeeee."

Vern kept on walking.

Maggie hopped on one foot to get her flip-flop adjusted. Then she ran down the warm asphalt road after him.

Mud

Every time Pap slammed on the brakes of the
Chevrolet, four things happened. The tail-gate
dropped, the sun visors flopped down, the glove
compartment opened, and Mud slid onto the
floor.

This time Mud was so surprised at the sudden
stop that he struck the tender part of his throat
on the door of the glove compartment. Then with
a yelp of pain he slid to the worn floor.

His throat felt as if something were caught
inside, and he gagged-coughed a few times. He
looked with interest at the small wad of spit he
had coughed up on the floor. Then he jumped
onto the seat to look around.

Pap was outside the truck. Mud jumped nimbly
out of the door and joined him. Pap paid no
attention to Mud, but Mud was used to that. Pap
knew he was there.

The next few moments were beyond Mud's
ability to understand. There was a crash, a shot,
and then a struggle that sent beer cans rolling
down the street and Mud under the Chevrolet.

When he realized that some men were struggling with Pap, hurting him, he darted out to
help. A kick from one of the policemen sent him

back under the truck. Stray cans shot at him, scared him, sent him further back.

He waited between the front wheels of the truck. He was panting with alarm, his ears flat on his broad head, his golden eyes wild.

After a moment he crawled on his belly to the driver's side of the truck. He thought it might be a good idea to get inside. The door had been closed.

Still keeping close to the pavement, he went to the back of the truck. He looked out. He didn't see Pap anywhere.

He was getting ready to jump into the truck and lie down on a gunnysack when the tow truck arrived. As soon as the huge hook clanged under the truck's bumper, Mud started running.

He ran right down the middle of Sumter Avenue, on the yellow line, his ears flying behind him, his tail low.

"That stupid dog's going to get hit!"

"Maybe he's rabid!"

"Someone ought to call the dog catcher."

Mud kept on running for five blocks until he came to an intersection, and then he turned left on a red light, causing curses and the squealing of brakes.

Mud was usually cautious about traffic because he had been hit by a car when he was six weeks old. That's how he had become Pap's dog in the first place. He and his mother—a big yellow farmer's dog named Minnie—had been chasing cars along County Road 26. His mother

46

was a great car chaser, and the first thing all her pups learned was to chase cars.

Mud had inherited from his mother a lot of natural ability for chasing cars, but he still had a lot to learn.

On that particular morning Mud and Minnie had spent a lot of time lying in the shade, waiting for the hum of a motor.

About noon Minnie heard a loud roar. It was a car Minnie particularly liked to chase, a BMW. She got up from her hole under the tree and jumped the ditch. Mud did too.

Minnie got down low in the weeds—she liked to take cars by surprise. Mud was beside her, down low too. His mother's body was trembling with excitement. His was too.

The car roared into view. Minnie and Mud sprang out of their hiding place.

But this time the car didn't gain speed as it usually did. This time it didn't race Minnie. This time it swerved right at her.

Minnie got out of the way with a graceful, twisting backward dive, but Mud didn't. Mud was hit and flung into a drainage ditch beside the road.

Pap came by about a half hour later, on foot. He was whistling "Camptown Races". He stopped after the first *doo-dah* because he saw Minnie. She was whining and taking anxious steps back and forth at the far side of the ditch.

It was clear to Pap she was worried about something in the ditch.

"Well, let's see what we got here," said Pap.

Mud was so covered with mud that Pap didn't see him at first. Then he said, "Well, well."

He put one foot down in the ditch, and he touched Mud's throat in a certain place to see if he was still alive. When he saw that he was, he said, "Let me help you, pal," in the same voice he would use if he was helping one of the children.

"Not another dog," the kids' mom had said when she saw him carrying Mud through the doorway.

Pap nodded.

"I wish one time you'd bring home something worth looking at, like a French poodle."

"Where'd you find him, Pap?" Vern asked.

"In the mud. His leg's broke."

"Well, as soon as it heals, you get rid of him. I mean it."

"I know you do."

Mud spent most of the afternoon running around town, dodging cars and trucks and people. At dusk he dropped like a bag of bones under the carryout window of a Dairy Queen. He lay there, so spent, so miserable, that during the evening people began dropping pieces of their hamburgers around him, the way people drop coins into a beggar's hat.

Here was the word he heard again and again, but even if someone had presented him with a sirloin steak, he would not have had the heart to eat it.

48

Busting Open

"What's wrong with you—really?" Junior asked. "I'm serious. I have to know." For two hours Junior had been trying to get Ralphie to tell him why he was in the hospital. "I told you what was wrong with me," Junior went on in a bargaining voice.

"No, you didn't. The nurse did."

Junior said, "Well, I would have."

"You'll find out when I go to therapy."

"What's therapy?"

"Don't you know anything?"

"I guess not." Junior sounded so low that Ralphie relented.

He said, "Oh, all right. Here is what's really and truly wrong with me. I swallowed water-melon seeds and now water-melons are growing inside me, and when they get big, I'm going to bust open."

"No," Junior said.

"When I bust open, you better get out of the way or you'll get water-melon and guts all over you."

"No!"

"After I bust open, they're going to put a zip in my stomach so I can zip myself open and shut."

"No!"

"Now, Ralphie." It was the nurse again—more little paper cups, more pills. "What lies are you telling Junior this time?"

"He told me he had water-melons inside him and marbles in his head. He told me he was going to bust open and then you were going to put a zip in him."

Junior tossed his pink pill down like a pro.

"Just don't listen to him, Junior. Don't believe a word he says. He's—"

"Excuse me."

Junior looked up in alarm. Everything about the hospital alarmed him, put him on his guard—trolleys, needles, hammers; and now a policeman was standing in the doorway. The only good thing so far about being in the hospital had been getting away from the police!

The policeman said exactly what Junior was afraid he would say: "Can I talk to the Blossom boy for a few minutes?"

"Me?" Junior asked. He pulled his covers up higher on his chest. He wanted to pull them over his head.

The policeman nodded and came into the room. "How are you feeling this morning, son?"

"I'm fine." Junior's voice was high and thin as a reed.

"Were you one of the policemen who was there when he fell?" Ralphie asked. He was turned on his side now, propped on his elbow, watching

50

with interest. He did not wear hospital gowns, and he had on a T-shirt that said Genius Inside.

The policeman said, "Yes."

"Then why didn't you catch him?"

"What?"

"When he fell, why didn't you catch him?" Ralphie spoke each word as carefully as if he were talking to someone who was dull-witted.

"It all happened pretty fast, son," the policeman said.

"Yeah, but you guys are supposed to be pretty fast, have quick reactions. What if it had been a burglary? If you can't move any quicker than that, you wouldn't even have your gun out till the robbers had escaped. Part of your training should be in fast reactions, *bang-bang*; and if you haven't got them, you should get a desk job or work in a cafeteria. On TV the cops—"

"We do our best, son." The policeman turned his back on Ralphie. "Are your legs giving you a lot of trouble?"

"No," Junior lied.

"They're broken," Ralphie told the policeman's back. "Sure, they're giving him trouble. You think it's fun to have broken legs?"

Junior kept his eyes on the mound his toes made under the sheet. He was very, very grateful to have Ralphie in the next bed. Ralphie was better than a lawyer, taking his side, bringing up points Junior had not even thought of. He would have given Ralphie a look of gratitude, but the policeman was standing between them.

51

"The reason I was out at your place yesterday afternoon," the policeman was saying, "was because earlier in the day we had to arrest your grandfather."

"Pap?" Now he looked at the policeman.

"Your grandfather was disturbing the peace. He pulled out a shotgun and fired it on Spring Street."

"Did he kill anybody?"

"No."

"Hit anybody?"

"No, but he's in gaol, and he's going to have to have a hearing. The hearing's day after tomorrow, and after that, depending on how things go, he's liable to spend a month or two in the county gaol."

"Pap? Gaol?" Junior couldn't fit the two pictures together. *"Pap? Gaol?"*

"He has a right to a court-appointed lawyer," Ralphie said. "By the way, did you read him his rights?"

The policeman ignored Ralphie and gave Junior a look of regret. He took out pencil and paper.

"Now, son, what we need to know is where your mom is and how to get in touch with her. Your grandfather—Pap, as you call him—told me there were two other kids, your brother and your sister"—he checked a notepad—"Maggie and Vern, and we need to know where they are."

Junior looked up at the policeman with his mouth hanging open. He couldn't have said a word if he'd wanted to. It was as if words hadn't even been thought of yet.

Ralphie leaned around the policeman. "Under the law," he said, "you aren't required to tell him—one—single—thing."

"Thank you," said Junior.

The Gaolbird

Maggie was at the bus stop, sitting on the bench that had been put there by the Parkinson Funeral Home. She was swinging her legs back and forth.

She wished, as she usually did, that she had on a pair of cowboy boots. Her mom had bought her lots of boots when she was little—Maggie even had a picture of herself coming home from the hospital with a pair of tiny cowboy boots sticking out from under the blanket.

But this year her mom had said, "Maggie, your feet are growing so fast, it would be wasting money."

"I can't go around without boots," Maggie had said. It was like going around undressed.

"They'd be too little in six months."

"Then buy me a big pair. I'll grow into them. Buy me a cheap pair at Shoe Mart."

"I don't even have the money for that, shug." Her mom's voice when she said the word *shug* always sounded so sad, so regretful, that Maggie could never keep on begging.

Maggie imagined how much better she would look if she had boots on now instead of worn green flip-flops. Cowboy boots made any outfit look classy, even a worn T-shirt and cut-off jeans.

Across the street her brother Vern was walking slowly up and down in front of the city gaol, pausing every now and then to give the secret bird-call. *Bobwhite! Bobwhite!* Four more steps. *Bobwhite!*

Vern was listening for an answering whistle from inside the gaol. This was the only way he could think of to find out if Pap was inside.

He whistled again and waited. His head was cocked to one side, like a bird's, listening.

Maggie thought Vern looked so suspicious, he would probably end up getting arrested himself. No one in his right mind stood in front of the city gaol whistling like a bobwhite.

She had said, "Well, it sounds stupid to me." And then because she couldn't think of anything better, she had added, "But go ahead and try it if you don't mind making a fool of yourself."

A bus came by, and the bus driver opened the door for her. "I'm not going anywhere," she called. As the door closed she added, "I wish I was."

The bus passed, and Maggie could see Vern again, at the last window now. She wished that she would look down in the gutter and spot a five-dollar bill. Then she'd go straight to a pay phone.

"Mom," she would say. "We have an emergency."

Bobwhite! Bobwhite!

Maggie was going to be a trick rider like her mom when she grew up. Her dad had been in the rodeo too. He had been World's Champion Single Steer Roper in 1973. He had won $6,259 that year, and they had thought they were on easy street.

The next year he had been killed by a steer in Ogallala, Nebraska, in a rodeo that Maggie could never remember. "Don't you remember us waiting for Mom to get back from the hospital?" Vern sometimes asked in amazement. "We hid under the stands."

"No."

"Don't you remember driving home with Mom crying so bad, she drove off the road every few miles?"

"No."

The truth was, Maggie didn't really want to remember. She scratched a mosquito bite on the back of her leg. Then she sat forward, watching her brother with new interest.

Vern was listening to something. He was standing there with one ear turned up to the last high window on the side of the gaol.

"Do you hear something?" Maggie called.

She waited until two cars passed, and she ran across the street to join him.

'Do you hear something or are you just acting like you do?"

Vern held up one hand to quiet her.

"I have a right to know if you heard something," she began, but then she stopped. She turned her head, ear up, to the window too.

From inside the gaol came the answering call of a bobwhite.

"He's in there!" Maggie said. She was as delighted as if she'd discovered he was in the movies. She grabbed Vern's arms and tried to swing him around. He was unyielding.

Bobwhite!

"He's in there, all right," Vern said.

"Well, let's go."

"Where?"

"To see him."

"Are you stupid or what? We can't go walking in the police station."

Bobwhite! Bobwhite! The bobwhite was getting excited now.

"Why not?"

"Because that's exactly what they expect us to do. That's why they didn't bother setting a trap for us at the farm. They knew we'd have to come down here. We walk in and—bam—they get us too."

Bobwhite! Bobwhite!

"Why would they want us, though? That's what I don't understand."

"All I know is that they do. They wouldn't have come to the farm, would they, if they hadn't wanted us? They wouldn't have taken Junior away, would they, if they didn't want him? What we got to find out is why."

"How are we going to do that?"

57

He held up his dynamited finger. "One. We got to find out what Pap's in gaol for." He held up another finger. "Two. We got to find out where Junior is. Three. We got to get them both out."

"How, Vern, how?"

"I'm thinking." And as Vern scratched his head with his dynamited finger, inside the gaol the bobwhite kept whistling and whistling and whistling.

With her flip-flop Maggie rubbed the mosquito bite on the back of her leg. "You better answer Pap. He's going to whistle his head off if you don't . . ."

Maggie trailed off as she looked up at Vern. He was watching her with such intensity that she swallowed. "What is it?" she asked. "What's wrong?"

"I just figured it out."

"What? What are you talking about?"

"We," he said, "are going to have to break into city gaol."

Pap's Place

Pap was standing on his bunk. His face was turned to the patch of light overhead, his window. With shaking fingers he was trying to reach the chain that opened the vent.

"What you trying to do, pops?" someone in the next cell asked. "Don't open the vent 'cause hot air'll come in. The good thing about this gaol is the AC."

"The only good thing," someone said down the way.

Pap's fingers trembled an inch below the chain. He stretched higher. Now he was a half inch away. His fingers made scissor movements under the chain.

Bobwhite! The call came again from the sidewalk below. Pap stopped stretching his old bones long enough to put his hand on his chest and answer.

Bobwhite!

"He think he a bird. Man, he think he gone fly out the window," another man said.

"*Byyyyye-bye, blackbird*," someone sang.

There was amused laughter. Everyone but Pap was a regular and knew one another. Two of them had been arrested together on a drunk and disorderly charge and were playing cards. Another was playing his Japanese transistor radio. Pap was not even aware they were in the same gaol with him.

"Gin!" a card player cried.

Up until the moment Pap had heard the call of the bobwhite, he had been in the deepest, blackest despair of his life. If he could have stopped himself from breathing, he would have. He would just have let all the air out of his lungs and not taken any more in. It would have been a relief to everybody and everything—to his worn-out lungs, the police, his disgraced family. *Good riddance* was the expression.

Then came the whistle. He had taught the kids that himself. "Here's what my brothers and me used to do when we wanted to call each other, like one would be in school and we'd want him to sneak out and go fishing with us and we'd do this: *Bobwhite! Bobwhite!*"

Vern had caught on right away and was now as good as Pap. Maggie was passable, and Junior was, as Pap put it, "getting there."

Hearing that whistle today had made tears come to his eyes and he hadn't cried in the four years since his son Cotton had died in Ogallala, Nebraska.

Hearing that whistle had been like hearing something from his past and something from his future at the same time. It was the first glimmer of hope Pap had felt since the gaol door clanked shut behind him.

In his excitement Pap had not bothered to wipe his tears away, and they were now making small paths down his dusty cheeks, falling easily into the wrinkles like raindrops into a gulley.

Pap's fingers reached again for the elusive chain. He actually touched the metal this time.

"What's he gone do when he gets up there? Ain't nobody skinny enough to get through that little bitty window."

Someone said, "Let him try. Maybe he like Rubber Man, in the funny papers."

Laughter.

"I wish I was the Invisible Man. You wouldn't see me around this place no more."

More laughter.

Pap looked around, not at the man who had spoken but at the man in the next cell who had his radio tuned to Rock 101. With all that racket it was a miracle he had heard the kid's whistle at all. And worse, the loud music might have prevented the kids from hearing his answering whistle.

"Turn that off," Pap said.

"I like it onnnnn." The man with the radio did not bother to open his eyes.

Pap looked up at the window again, then back to the man, then back to the window, bewildered about what to do next.

He heard nothing. Maybe they'd given up. Maybe at this moment they were walking home.

The rock song ended, and in the relative quiet

of a commercial Pap heard a bobwhite whistle. It sounded fainter, as if the kids were moving away.

In a desperate move Pap yanked up his mattress. He rolled it into a wad and stood on it. His high-top shoes dug into the filling.

Now he could reach the chain. He pulled it open. Warm air rushed into his face, along with the sounds of a bobwhite. Pap threw back his head and gave the answering whistle ten times without stopping.

"He crazy," one of the card players said.

And no one in city gaol bothered to argue with the card player.

Ralphie Goes to Therapy

Junior was sleepy, but every time his eyes closed he snapped them open. He had to stay awake. He didn't want to miss it when Ralphie went to therapy. Finding out what was wrong with Ralphie was the only thing he had to look forward to.

And yet, like everything in this whole hospital, in this whole world, it would probably be a disappointment. Like lunch. The memory brought tears to Junior's eyes.

All morning long Junior had been looking forward to lunch. When the nurse put his tray down and rolled up his bed and he saw a huge hamburger, he could have jumped up and down with joy—if, of course, it had not been for the broken legs.

He had just picked up the hamburger, which he intended to devour in exactly four bites. A boy in his school was famous for eating a whole hamburger in one bite—Junior had seen him do it. Then the boy would drink his whole milk in one pull on the straw, put his cookies—however many—in his mouth, and go out to recess.

Junior wasn't that good yet. Four bites was his record. He was just getting ready for the first bite when Ralphie said, "You aren't going to eat that stuff without testing it first, are you?"

Junior stopped with the hamburger at his lips. The smell of the bun had made his mouth water. "Why would I test it?"

"Stupid, to make sure they haven't put medicine in it."

"Medicine." Junior looked down at his hamburger. He closed his mouth.

"Yeah, drugs, you know, to keep you groggy, so they can do things to you."

"Do they really do that?"

"You better believe it."

Junior wasn't as hungry as he thought he was. "Maybe I'll just drink my milk."

"Is it chocolate?"

"Yes."

"Then be double careful."

"Why?" Junior put his milk carton back on his tray, exactly in the little wet square where it had been.

"That's usually their first target. They figure, see, that the kid's going to go for chocolate milk. He probably doesn't get that at home. 'Wow, chocolate milk!' And down the hatch without half tasting it. Either that or the ice-cream. Why do you think you get ice-cream every single meal?"

Junior didn't know they did. He folded his hands over his chest.

He looked at the items on his tray. It was a nice tray, better than at the school cafeteria.

Getting a tray this nice had given him a special feeling.

At school Junior had always had to bring his lunch in a paper bag, and he envied the kids that went through the line and got trays. Now he had thought he was part of that happy privileged group at last.

"What do these drugs taste like?" he asked.

He glanced over at Ralphie. He saw Ralphie was eating his hamburger.

"If it's poison—" Junior began.

"I didn't say poison," Ralphie corrected through a mouthful of hamburger. "I said drugs."

To Junior it was the same thing. "If it's got drugs in it, then why are you eating it?"

"I'm an addict. I need it. It's my fix."

After a long moment Junior picked up one potato chip. He figured it would be hard to get drugs into a potato chip. He progressed slowly, though, nibbling the edges. Maybe it did taste funny.

The nurse came in. She said, "I thought you were so hungry, Junior."

"Not really."

He wondered if he should swallow the funny-tasting potato chip or spit it out.

Ralphie said, "He's scared there's drugs in the food."

"I wonder who could have put that idea in his head," the nurse said. "Junior, your food is not drugged."

"Of course *she'd* say that," Ralphie said.

65

"Would you like me to take a bite of your hamburger?"

Junior nodded.

She broke off a piece and ate it. "Anything else?"

"The milk."

"Well, let me get a straw. Honestly, Ralphie, we're going to have to put you in isolation. You get meaner by the day." She took a sip of milk. "Now do you think you can eat something?"

Junior nodded.

"I'll be back for your trays later."

As she went from the room, Ralphie said, "Sure, she tasted the hamburger and the milk, but she didn't taste the ice-cream. You had better hand that over to me."

"No way!"

Now as he lay waiting for Ralphie to go to therapy, he wondered if he had made a serious mistake in eating the ice-cream. It had not tasted the way he remembered ice-cream tasting.

And he did feel drugged. His eyelids were so heavy, he could not keep them from dropping over his eyes. And he couldn't think straight.

"What time do you go?" he asked drowsily.

"Where?"

"Therapy."

"I've already been, stupid! I'm back."

Junior didn't know whether it was true or not. He couldn't open his eyes to find out.

Junior slept.

Gaolbreak

"Break *into* gaol!" Maggie yelled.

"Shut up! You want the police to hear you?"

Maggie lowered her voice. "Break *into* gaol? Are you out of your mind? We cannot break *into* gaol."

"Yes, we can. Look, it's not like breaking into a bank. The police expect people to break into banks. They have alarms set for people breaking into banks."

"They have alarms in gaol, too."

"They have alarms for breaking *out* of gaol. There's a big difference. Nobody is expecting anybody to break *into* gaol. That would be stupid."

"Exactly."

"Maggie, listen—we have to. There's no other way we can talk to Pap."

"Why don't we call him on the phone?"

"Now you're the one who's out of her mind. You think they let prisoners take phone calls?"

"They let them have one. I saw it on TV."

"Make one. They let them make one—to their lawyer. There's a big difference."

"No way," Maggie said. 'I am not breaking into gaol."

"All right, you don't have to go. If you're scared, you can wait here. That might be better. Then if I get caught, you'll still be free to help us."

"Vern, couldn't we write him a letter?"

"A letter! Don't you think they open every single letter that comes in the gaol? What's your next idea, Maggie—that we bake him a cake with a file in it?"

Tears stung Maggie's eyes. She was tired. She wanted to be home in her bed instead of in front of the city gaol.

"I want Mom."

"You think I don't?"

Vern's thin shoulders sagged. He sighed. He jammed his hands deep in his pockets. He said, "All right, you might as well know the worst."

"The worst?" Maggie swung her head around so fast her braids whipped around her neck. "What worst could there be?"

"Here it is. I tried to call Mom three days ago and she wasn't where she was supposed to be. The Paisano Motel had never heard of her. There's no way in the world we can reach Mom now. Mom's gone."

As soon as Vern said "Mom's gone" Maggie began to sob. She didn't bother covering her eyes. She just threw back her head and bawled.

"Shut up, Maggie. Come on, shut up!" He decided yelling at her wasn't going to work. He lowered his voice. "Please, Maggie, listen. Be quiet. They'll hear you inside the station."

68

He drew her down the sidewalk away from the door. She followed, her eyes blind with tears. They stopped beneath an elm tree.

"Maggie, please don't cry. Please. You'll make yourself sick. You won't have to go in the gaol if you don't want to, and if I don't think it's going to work, if I'm not absolutely sure, I won't go in either."

Maggie kept crying. It was such a relief to be getting some sympathy that she couldn't have stopped if she had wanted to.

"Maggie," he said finally in one last desperate attempt, "I'll buy you some cowboy boots if you stop."

She blinked. "You don't have any money."

"I do."

"With you?"

"Yes."

"How much?"

"Twenty-two dollars and seventy-seven cents."

He remembered suddenly that he had spent three dollars and thirty cents on the incompleted phone call to their mother, but there was no need to mention that. "Pap gave it to me for helping collect pop cans."

"Is that enough for boots?"

"Cheap boots."

Maggie hesitated.

"But the cheap boots look nice, Maggie; even cowboys can't tell them from the expensive ones."

Maggie wiped her tears on her arm.

"Tell me what we're going to do," she said.

More Mud

The Dairy Queen was closed. The lights were out. The parking lot was empty.

Still Mud lay where he had fallen, beneath the carryout window. He was like a character in a fairy tale who had been put under a wicked, hurtful spell. Around him were the dried offerings of strangers.

The only movement was an occasional twitching of his long, dusty legs. Mud was running in his dreams.

It was the silence that brought Mud to his senses. As long as people had been fussing over him, begging him to eat—"Come on, boy, it's hamburger. See, hamburger!"—it had been easy to lie there, out of it, too unhappy to move. Even when a boy had lifted Mud's lip and poked a piece of bacon cheeseburger inside, Mud had not reacted.

"Don't do that!" the boy's mother had cried, swatting at the boy and hitting Mud.

Mud did not flinch.

Another swat. This time the mother hit her mark, the back of the boy's trousers. "Didn't I tell you not to fool with strange dogs? You want to get rabies?"

70

"Nooooooooooooooo . . ."

Now the parking lot was so quiet, Mud could have been the only living creature left in the world. He was awake, and he knew he was going to have to open his eyes.

He opened one. He rolled it up to the Dairy Queen, down to the streetlight.

Then he lifted his head and looked around. He saw nothing that looked familiar. He could not even remember lying down here.

He was not hungry, but it was easier to swallow the scrap of bacon cheeseburger that was already in his mouth than to spit it out. The scrap hit his empty stomach, causing real hunger.

Still he was selective. He ignored all bread that smelt of mayonnaise and all french fries. He separated pickles, onions, tomato, and lettuce from meat and made a discard pile before eating the meat. He ended the meal with a little chocolate shake which someone had thoughtfully poured in the lid of the cup. He licked the excess from his whiskers.

Mud shook himself, stretched, and lifted his leg in the direction of the Dairy Queen. Then he went to the kerb and looked both ways. The street was deserted. He ambled to the corner.

There Mud hesitated. He stood with his nose high, smelling the evening air. He took a few steps to the right, then to the left, figuring out which smells came from which direction.

Mud reached a decision. He lifted his leg on

71

the telephone pole, and then, with a sort of ambling gait, he set off in the direction of town.

Mud was a one-man dog. He could not even remember his pre-Pap days when he and Minnie had chased cars, when the farm girls down the road had dressed him and his brother up in doll's clothes and played baby with them.

"How's your baby today?"

"It's sick."

"Mine's sick too."

And he and his brother ate medicine made of grass until they could escape and run through the yard, tripping on their dresses.

Mud's life began when Pap reached down into the ditch and took his shivering body in his gentle hands.

In all the years since Mud had recovered from the accident, Pap had taken him everywhere he went. If Pap went to the barn, Mud went to the barn. If Pap got in the truck, Mud got in. On the rare occasions when Pap said "Stay," Mud waited in the back of the truck, curled up on a gunny-sack, with his ears turning radar-like for the sound of Pap's shuffling feet.

His job in life, as nearly as he could figure it out, was keeping Pap company.

Now his job was even clearer. He had to find Pap.

He crossed the deserted street, pausing on the yellow line to sniff the evening air.

Visitors

All the things Junior wanted to invent had already been invented. It was the story of his life. He would say, "I'm going to invent shoes with little wheels on the bottom," and before he could describe how people would roll around like magic on the wheeled shoes, Vern would sneer, "And what are you going to call them—roller-skates?" Then Junior would remember where he had got the idea.

He had, at various times, wanted to invent motorbikes, pogo sticks, and the harmonica.

"I'm going to invent a tiny little musical instrument, like a sideways horn, that you blow in, and you can slide it up and down and get different notes."

"Why don't you call it a harmonica?" Another of Vern's sneers.

That night, after supper, Junior remembered with tears in his eyes that he had once almost invented the harmonica. What made him remember was that Ralphie's two little brothers came to see him and one of them brought Ralphie a tiny harmonica exactly one inch long. He had bought the harmonica in a joke store.

As soon as Ralphie began to wheeze out a tune

on the harmonica, tears came to Junior's eyes. It wasn't only that some inventor had had the idea first and beat him to it. It was that no one had brought him a tiny harmonica. Nobody had brought him anything.

And he didn't have any visitors. He was never going to have any. Maggie and Vern didn't even know where he was. And if they did come, they wouldn't think to bring him a tiny harmonica.

As he lay there, wiping his tears on his top sheet, listening to an off-key chorus of "Dixie" from the next bed, he suddenly wished he had told the policeman where to find Vern and Maggie.

He wished he had said to the policeman, "Look behind the house in the woods. They have a hideout by the ravine." No, he wished he had told the policeman to go in the woods and give the whistle of a bobwhite, and when Vern and Maggie ran out, thinking it was him, the police could grab them.

He wished he had thought to say, "You better bring them here for identification." He wanted to give them a hard, unforgiving look before they were led away to prison.

"What's wrong with you?" one of Ralphie's brothers asked. The brother had been lying in the empty bed across from Junior, pretending he had appendicitis. Now he was sitting up, cross-legged.

While Junior was deciding whether he could tell his story without starting to sob, Ralphie switched his harmonica into his cheek and chanted, "He fell off a roof. He was trying to fly. He hit the ground. He thought he would die. A poem, by Ralph Waldo Smith." Then he blew one loud, piercing chord, that used every hole on the harmonica.

After that, having had the whole thing turned into a poem, followed by what sounded like a musical raspberry, Junior didn't feel like saying anything.

"You know what? Now nobody in your family will ever be allowed up on the roof again," the brother said. "Ralphie fell of the riding lawn mower five years ago and cut off his leg and none of us have been allowed on the riding mower since. We can't even sit on it when it's in the garage. Just because *he* was stupid enough to fall off, *we* have to be punished the rest of our lives."

Junior wiped his tears on his sheet, this time because he wanted to get a closer look at Ralphie's brother. "Is that what happened to him?" He nodded his head in the direction of Ralphie's bed.

"Yes. What did he tell you—that a crocodile bit off his leg at Disneyland?"

"He didn't tell me anything."

"That's what he usually tells people, but he's never even been to Disneyland. He fell off a mower, and the mower cut off his leg."

"And," the other brother said, moving into the conversation, "he's had five operations because his bone keeps poking through. He just had one, and now he's getting a new leg. Every time he grows, he has to get a new leg. There's his old one over in the corner. You want to see it?"

Junior nodded.

The brothers had a short tug-of-war with the leg to see who would have the honour of bringing it to Junior. The bigger brother won and ran over to Junior's bed. He laid the leg on Junior's lap and sat on the side of the bed, jiggling up and down.

Junior didn't even feel the pain of having his legs bounced. On his lap was Ralphie's leg. Ralphie's leg!

"Big mouth," sneered Ralphie from the next bed. "When I get my new leg, the first thing I'm going to use it for is to kick your guts out."

Walking the Plank

"Hand up the board."

Vern was up in the crook of the elm tree by the gaol. Maggie was below him, hiding a ten-foot board between her and the trunk of the tree.

"Someone's coming," she hissed.

"Look innocent," he hissed back.

"I am innocent!"

The man walked slower as he saw Maggie flattened against the tree. When she saw he was going to stop, her eyes got as round as cartoon eyes.

"Oh, hello." She pulled her lips up into a smile.

The man combed his hair with his hands. "Are you all right?"

"Of course."

"It's late, isn't it, for you to be out by yourself?"

"Yes, but my dad's a cop. He'll be out in a minute. He told me to wait here. I'm not supposed to go inside because children aren't allowed. My dad thinks criminals are a bad influence."

"Do you want me to go in and tell your dad you're out here?"

"He knows," Maggie said quickly. Behind her the board began falling forward, and she stopped it with her head. She looked up at the man through her eyelashes.

The man watched Maggie and the board for a full thirty seconds. Maggie shoved the board back against the tree with her head and stared right back at him.

Overhead, in the tree, Vern waited without breathing. Ever since he had gotten the idea of breaking into gaol, he had been gripped by a kind of excitement he had never felt before. He was amazed that his ordinary, everyday mind had thought of it. Breaking *into* gaol!

It had come to him in a flash. One moment he had been standing there with Maggie, looking stupidly at the gaol, wondering what to do, and the next moment the idea burst out of his brain like one of those fantastic Dr Seuss trees, too wild and wonderful to be real.

He gazed down through the leaves where the man stood with Maggie. He could see the man's bald spot. Vern took a deep breath and closed his eyes in prayer.

Finally the man remembered when he and his gang used to steal lumber at night to build a clubhouse. With a smile, he shrugged and went on down the street.

Again Maggie got ready to pass the board up to Vern. "Here," she said. When she felt him take the board, she put her hands on the bottom and boosted it the rest of the way.

"I got it," Vern said. "Let go."

Maggie moved back into the shadows by the gaol and watched. The only sound was the rustling of elm leaves as Vern and the board made their way up the tree. The rustling stopped across from the open vent of the gaol.

Slowly the board appeared from the side of the tree. Slowly it extended across the sidewalk. Slowly it waved up and down like one end of a see-saw.

"You're too low," Maggie called. "You're going to miss it by a mile."

The end of the board scraped against the side of the gaol. It was about five feet below the vent. It rose shakily in the air. Then it wavered, trembled, turned sideways, and clattered down to the sidewalk.

"Verrrrn," Maggie said.

"I didn't do it on purpose," he snapped from inside the tree.

"Well, that could have hit me."

The only answer was the rustling of leaves as Vern made his way down.

Maggie got the board and dragged it back to the tree trunk. She waited for Vern's "Hand it up."

"Here."

"I got it."

"Be careful this time."

Maggie was glad she had had the last word. She went back and stood in the shadows, this time far out of the way of the elm tree.

Again she heard the rustling of leaves, again she saw the board coming out like a gangplank.

"Too high," Maggie called.

Vern groaned and heaved and shoved, and by a miracle—that was how it seemed to Maggie— the board swept across the gap and landed on the ledge. It snapped into place as neatly as something from a Lego building set.

"Now," Maggie called, "all you have to do is walk across."

"That's all," Vern echoed.

Up in the tree he eyed the narrow board, and his heart sank. Vern had never admitted it, but he had always been aware that he did not have the daring his brother and sister had. Junior wanted to be a stunt man, Maggie wanted to be a trick rider, and he wanted to do something no one in the family had ever done—work in an office.

He dreamed of sharp pencils and unlimited stacks of paper and paper clips and rulers. His happiest moments in school came when the teacher asked them to fill out forms. That, he felt, was the closest he had ever come to office work. He handed in the neatest forms of anyone in his class.

That's why it was such a miracle that he had not only conceived this brilliant, ingenious plan but was putting it into effect.

He stepped on the board. He jiggled to make sure it was steady.

Maggie saw the shaking leaves and called, "Be careful. Don't fall, whatever you do."

Vern did not answer. He put his right foot in front of his left, heel to toe, then took one more step. He was holding on to the overhead branches, working on balance. He took another step. Another.

Then the branches stopped. Vern stood for a moment, holding the last two leaves, one in each hand. Then, with a sigh, he let go.

He held his arms out to the side. No circus tightrope walker had ever concentrated harder.

Vern kept his eyes on the vent. Heel to toe, toe to heel, he made his way across the board. His arms see-sawed gently in the cool night air. He did not look down once.

Below, Maggie stood with her hands clasped. She appeared to be, and was, praying.

"We need Junior for this," she said.

"Thanks," Vern said through tight lips.

The board was beginning to sag. With every step it bent lower, buckling under his weight. Ahead he could see that the board was slipping closer to the end of the ledge. He took another heel-to-toe step.

The board sagged lower.

"Vern," Maggie called. "Did you notice that the board's starting to bend?"

Vern did not answer. He figured that one more step was all the board could take. One more step, and he and the board would crash to the pavement.

At that awful moment, with his arms waving at his sides, his heart pounding in his throat, the vent going in and out of focus before his tear-filled eyes, Vern made the decision of his life.

Vern jumped.

Travelling Mud

Mud was making his way through the finest section of town, Maple Leaf Manor, where the rich people lived. He loped along the smooth white sidewalks, taking his time, pausing now and then to lift his leg on a wrought-iron mailbox or a particularly fine piece of shrubbery.

An occasional car passed, lighting up his pale fur, giving a red look to his golden eyes. Mud paid the cars no attention.

He slowed. His sharp ears had picked up the sound of running water. It came from behind this house, and he turned on to the soft manicured lawn. He ambled around the house to the swimming pool, where a spray of water ran continuously down the silver sliding board.

He stretched out on the cool tiles around the pool, stuck his head over the side, and lapped the clear chlorinated water. It wasn't as good as toilet water or creek water, which he was accustomed to, but Mud was thirsty.

When he had drunk all he wanted, he spent a few seconds licking stray drops from his legs and feet. He chewed a flea on his ankle.

Then Mud got to his feet. He stretched. He was getting ready to lift his leg in the direction of a lounge chair to mark the fact that he'd been there.

Suddenly, from the right, Mud heard a long, low "*Rrrrrrr.*"

The hair rose on Mud's back. His sharp eyes looked in the shadows of a small walkway between the double garage and the house.

There Mud could see the high pointed ears of a Doberman. He could see the gleam of long white teeth.

The Doberman drew in enough breath to give another, longer "*Rrrrrrrrrrrrr.*" An answering growl rose in Mud's throat.

The Doberman leapt forward, throwing himself at Mud. He choked on his chain and fell back. He tried to attack again.

Mud hesitated. Mud had never started a fight in his life, but Mud had never run from a fight either.

Now he was ready for battle. His teeth were bared. His hair was up. His eyes were bright. If the Doberman got free, Mud would meet him more than half-way.

The Doberman was barking wildly, throwing himself in Mud's direction, trying either to break his chain or to pull the whole house down. Between leaps the metal links rattled against the slate floor.

"Franklin!" a voice called from an upstairs window. "Be quiet down there."

"Maybe it's a burglar, Sam."

"All right, already. I'll take a look."

84

Mud stood still, frozen at the edge of the pool. The patio lights went on. Mud lowered his tail. He heard sounds at the door: the unsnapping of the dead-bolt lock, the click of the doorknob. Franklin was barking wildly, knowing his owner was on the way. He was facing the door now, legs stiff with anticipation.

As the door opened, Mud ran around the pool. He whipped through the hedge and galloped across the lawn like a racehorse.

Behind him a voice said kindly, "What's wrong, Franklin? You all right, boy?"

Franklin whined with pleasure.

"Was some stray dog after your bone?"

Mud hit the sidewalk and slowed. He lifted his leg on a bush at the Doberman's driveway, then he took the time to scratch the grass vigorously with his back feet. A spray of fine zoysia grass flew into the night air.

Then, without a backward glance, Mud ambled down the sidewalk, on his way to Pap.

The Missing Harmonica

Junior could not get to sleep. The lights in his
room had been turned out. The hospital hall was
as quiet as it ever got. Ralphie had gone to sleep
with the little harmonica in his mouth, and every
time he breathed out, he played a soft, soothing
chord. Still Junior could not sleep.

Usually the only time Junior had trouble
sleeping was Christmas Eve. Even the times
when his mother had the terrible Christmas Eve
talks with them, warning in her quiet way that
sometimes Santa couldn't bring everything
everybody wanted.

Even when she looked directly at him during
the terrible talk, and he knew, knew deep in his
bones, that it was he who was not going to get
the bicycle, he still could not sleep from
excitement.

This was different. It was the opposite of
excitement. They did a lot of opposites in
school. The teacher would say, "The opposite of
day is—"

"Night!" Junior would cry.

"The opposite of lost is—"

"Found!"

Junior had never missed a single one. Some-

86

times he was a little bit slower than the rest of the class, but he had never missed one.

This was impossible, though, he thought. He went over it again. "The opposite of excitement is—"

There was only one answer: "Lying in the hospital with hurt legs."

And his legs did hurt. They had not hurt much during the day, and they had stopped hurting entirely when he had held Ralphie's artificial leg and worked the knee. He had even for one brief moment wanted a leg exactly like the one on his lap.

Now, however, his legs were making up for lost time. They hurt a lot.

He realized suddenly how much he loved the sounds of his own house. He missed them. Mud drinking loudly out of the toilet, Pap grinding his teeth, the wind chimes they had given their mom for her birthday clicking musically on the porch below, the occasional chinaberry dropping on the tin roof.

He felt so miserable that he reached for the buzzer beside his pillow. "Use this, Junior, if you need anything," the nurse had told him, but he never had. Ralphie spent a lot of time ringing his buzzer, demanding Cokes and candy over the intercom as if he were the president of the hospital. When the nurses ignored him, he pressed the buzzer and made terrible gagging noises or pretended to be choking.

Now Junior looked at his buzzer. He pressed the button. A voice on the intercom said, "Yes?"

"It's me—Junior," he answered miserably.

"Speak up, please."

"It's me—Junior."

"What's wrong, Junior?"

"I don't feel good."

"Do your legs hurt?"

"Yes."

"I'll bring you an aspirin."

"Thank you," he said politely. It was hard not to be polite to a voice coming from the wall.

But when the nurse arrived with the paper cup and the pill, he was crying too hard to swallow. "I want Maggie," he wailed. "I want Pap. I want Vern. I want my mommmmmmmm!"

"Will you shut him up?" Ralphie said, flipping over in disgust. "Where does he think he is—at a hog-calling contest?"

The nurse wrapped her arms around Junior and hugged him. He tried to pretend they were his mom's arms, but it didn't work. Still, he was glad to have arms of any sort around him. "Tomorrow, you know what you're going to do?" the nurse asked kindly.

He shook his head against her.

"You're going to get up and sit in a wheelchair and you can go down to the TV room, and you can roll up and down the hall, and the play lady comes with games and books and you can pick anything you want."

"Is that true?" Junior asked.

"Big deal," Ralphie sneered.

"Go to sleep, Ralphie. You—"

Ralphie clutched his throat. "I swallowed my harmonica."

"Come on, Ralphie, it's too late at night for that kind of foolishness."

"I swallowed my harmonica, I tell you! I'm not kidding! I really swallowed my harmonica! Where is it if I didn't swallow it?"

He began to pull at his pyjamas, frantically searching the wrinkles. He tore his pyjama top open and shook it. He lifted his pillow.

The nurse crossed to Ralphie's bed. "Let's take a look. It probably fell down in your covers." She pulled them back and searched among the wrinkled sheets. "Roll over." She ran her hands under him.

"He did have it in his mouth," Junior said helpfully. "It blew a note every time he breathed out."

"Ralphie, it looks like you'd have better sense than to go to sleep with a harmonica in your mouth. If I have to send you down to X-ray, and there's no harmonica inside you, I'm going to be—" she shook the top sheet so hard, it billowed and snapped, "—furious."

"If you swallow a harmonica, do they have to cut you open to get it out?" Junior asked.

"Nobody's cutting me open!" The words burst from Ralphie. His hands folded into fists. "I'm not going to let anybody cut me open. The doctor

89

promised me this was the last time I would have to—"

"There," the nurse said, "is your harmonica."

"Where?"

The nurse bent and picked something off the floor. She extended her hand. "There."

Ralphie looked at it suspiciously. "It doesn't look like my harmonica. How do you know it's mine?"

"Because nobody else on this floor has an inch-long harmonica. Now, I'm putting this in my pocket, Ralphie, and you can have it when you leave the hospital."

"I don't want it any more."

"I do," said Junior quickly.

"Take it," said Ralphie turning away from them.

"All right, you can have it when you leave the hospital," the nurse said. "And do you want this pill or not?"

"I don't need it any more," Junior said truthfully. The thought of owning his own harmonica was pain-killer enough.

Before he went to sleep, Ralphie said, "I knew it was on the floor all the time. I just wanted to scare her."

"And you did," Junior answered.

Breaking in

Pap was not asleep and he heard the noise of the board thumping into place against the vent over his head. He dared not hope it was the children, and yet he could feel his heart begin to race in his chest.

He stood up. Pap had to stand up in stages. He stood up first in a stoop, and when his legs got used to that, he straightened the rest of the way up.

Now he stood tall beside his bunk, his head straining painfully towards the window, his old neck twisted like a rooster's. He heard nothing. With his head back, his Adam's apple stuck out as far as his sagging chin.

He said softly, "Kids?"

No answer.

"Kids?"

He wanted to whistle, but the man in the next cell had threatened to kill him if he whistled like—the man did not know birdcalls—like a nuthatch one more time. Pap wasn't afraid of the man, but he didn't want a disturbance of any kind just now.

He heard a new noise. He couldn't place it. A soft silk-smooth sound overhead. He held his breath. He waited. He knew in his bones that the sound had something to do with him.

Everybody else in the gaol was asleep, snoring, snorting, groaning in their dreams. And they had gone to sleep instantly, because none of them was expecting anyone to drop in. Pap was, and so he alone waited alert in his lighted cell.

Even though he still couldn't place the thump, followed by the soft sliding sound, he knew it was his. His daddy used to have a saying long ago: "That piece of pie's got my name on it," and that was exactly the way Pap felt about the soft sliding noise overhead.

He waited with his hands twitching at his sides, his fingers making little beckoning movements.

The door opened, and a policeman came in for his hourly check. It was twelve o'clock.

The policeman walked slowly down the room, looking in each cell. He paused at Pap's cell. He looked Pap over from his shoes to his uncombed head. Pap's heart stopped beating.

"You better lie down, sir, get some sleep," the policeman said.

"I will. I will."

"You got a big day tomorrow."

"What?"

"Isn't your hearing tomorrow?"

"My what?"

"Your hearing."

"Oh, my hearing."

Pap nodded. He slumped to his bunk to get rid

of the policeman. He lay down. He pretended to close his eyes. Through a slit in his left eye he could see the policeman was still there.

He couldn't hear the soft sliding noises because the blood was pounding so hard in his head, it blocked out everything else.

"You a baseball fan?"

"What?" Pap's eyes snapped open. He was so filled with hope and dread and pounding blood, he couldn't even remember what baseball was. "Yes. No."

"Which is it?" The policeman smiled.

"Yes."

"Well, the Cards won. Braves won. Phillies lost."

"Oh."

Pap pulled back his lips in a smile. He swallowed so hard, his Adam's apple bobbed up to his chin.

Now at last, the policeman was moving back down the cells and into the office. The door closed.

With a sigh of relief Pap started to get to his feet. He was at the first, bent-knee stage, when he heard the noises outside.

There were three of them: a muffled scream, a soft thud against the side of the building, and then a long, loud clanging noise as something hit the sidewalk. It clattered, and then there was silence.

Pap scrambled on to his bunk.

"What's happened?" he called to the vent. "What's happened?"

He waited with his mouth open, like a thirsty man waiting for raindrops.

"What's happened? Please, somebody tell me what's happened!"

His feet were digging into his thin mattress, his hands gripping the concrete wall. It looked exactly like he was climbing up the wall, except that he wasn't getting any higher.

"What's happened?"

There was a long pause. Minutes went by. Pap was so still, he could hear the ticking of his pocket watch. Then Pap saw the most beautiful sight of his life. A hand came through the vent and clutched the sill.

"Vern," he asked, still not daring to hope, "is that you?"

"It's me," Vern answered.

Maggie Alone

Maggie was still waiting on the sidewalk, looking up at the lighted vent with her mouth open.

If she lived to be a hundred, she would never forget Vern's desperate leap for the building. He had flung himself through the air, his arms and legs churning like an Olympic jumper's. Then he slammed into the wall, and his thin hands gripped the ledge. He had hung there for what seemed to Vern and Maggie to be the longest minute and a half in the history of recorded time.

Maggie kept waiting for him to fall to the ground. Vern kept hanging there.

Maggie glanced around. She wished she had something to put under him to break his fall.

When Maggie saw the board, she got a brainstorm, the first of her life. "Hold on," she yelled.

She took the fallen board, upended it, shoved it up against the wall, and gave Vern's dangling feet a boost. It was all Vern needed.

One foot found a toehold. His other knee pushed his body out from the wall. He worked the toe of his shoe between the bricks, and he pulled himself up six inches. His toe moved up a brick.

Vern inched his way up the rest of the wall,

moving as carefully as a mountain climber, his tennis shoes digging into the wall, his hands reaching into the vent. It was a slow, super-human, agonising effort that Maggie watched from directly below.

She watched Vern wiggle eel-like through the vent. He had to turn his head sideways, the vent was so small, and she turned her head sideways too. She had sucked in her breath as he, too, had done to get his chest through the vent. She pulled in her stomach as he went over the sill.

For a few seconds there had been just his thin legs sticking out of the vent. Then they disappeared in a scissors kick, and Vern was in the city gaol.

The leap had been so exciting, and her part in it so spectacular, that Maggie had wanted to jump up and down and cheer. It had been like something out of the circus, the most exciting, successful moment of her entire life.

Now, however, with the realization that Vern was inside with Pap and that she was outside with nobody, all she felt was lonely.

"Vern!" she called softly.

It had been ten minutes since Vern's legs had disappeared.

"Vern?"

Tears came to her eyes and spilled on to her cheeks. Usually when Maggie cried, she wiped her tears away with the ends of her braids. It was the best part of having braids. That and crossing them under her nose and making a moustache. Those were the only two reasons she went to all the trouble of making the braids. Now she was too miserable to care.

"Vern?"

Far above her, in the light of the vent, Vern's small, round face appeared. Maggie lifted her arms like a mother urging her child to jump.

Vern said just one sentence before he slipped back into the gaol and out of sight.

"Junior's in Alderson General Hospital."

In the gaol Vern tumbled once again into Pap's trembling arms, and the two of them sat down on the side of Pap's bunk. The first few minutes of the reunion had been spent with Pap rubbing his hands over Vern, testing to make sure he was real, mumbling, "I knew you'd come. I knew you wouldn't let me down."

The next minutes were spent realizing that now instead of having one family member in gaol, they had two. After that, they hadn't said anything, just sat enjoying the comfort of each other's presence.

Finally Vern had broken the silence with "Maggie's outside."

"That's what I figured," Pap said.

Pap knew it wouldn't be proper to bring a girl into the men's half of city gaol. Then, with a sudden lift of heart, he remembered Junior.

Junior had been worrying Pap ever since the policeman had told him Junior was in the hospital. Now the heavy lines between Pap's brows eased. Things were working out all right after all. Maggie could take care of Junior.

"I'll boost you up, and you yell out and tell her Junior's in Alderson General Hospital."

"That's all?"

"She'll know what to do."

Vern had climbed on Pap's old sloping shoulders, turned his head sideways, poked it through the vent, and looked down at Maggie's pale face far below.

He called, "Junior's in Alderson General Hospital." Then he shinnied down Pap's body as if it were a tree, and joined him on the bunk.

No one in the gaol had awakened.

Pap, comforted at last, leaned back against the concrete block wall. Vern did too. Their eyes closed.

Vern opened his eyes. "I forgot something. Boost me up again, Pap."

"Verrrrrrrrrn," Maggie wailed. She stood with her head back like a howling dog. "What am I supposed to do nowwwwww?"

She looked down at the board at her feet. Maybe she could get it up the tree and across the gap to the ledge so Vern could come back across. She knew she couldn't. It had taken all her strength to lift it up for that one short boost. Maybe she could do something terrible and get arrested. "Just put me in with my family," she would tell the arresting officer, "—the Blossoms." She would look so pitiful that—

At that moment, with tears of pity welling in her eyes, Maggie heard the clink of a coin at her feet. She brushed her tears away with her braids.

The clink was followed by another. Then money poured from the vent. It fell around her like rain—nickels, dimes, pennies, wadded-up dollar bills.

Even before the last coin hit the sidewalk, Maggie was on her hands and knees, gathering it in.

Rich and Special

Maggie felt better. It was surprising how much more wonderful things looked when you were rich.

The money was in her jeans pocket—nineteen dollars and forty-nine cents. She had wrapped it up like a package, securely, with the dollar bills folded around the coins.

"Isn't it late for you to be out by yourself?" the bus driver asked.

Maggie was sitting on the long sideways seat behind him. Now that she had money, everything seemed to be going her way.

The bus had stopped. She had said, "By any chance do you go past Alderson Hospital?"

The bus driver had said, "I sure do."

She said, "How much?"

He said, "Fifty."

She said, "Just a minute." She unwrapped her package of money, dropped the money in the slot, and here she was, on her way.

Life sure was easy when you had money.

"I asked," the bus driver said again, "isn't it late for you to be out by yourself?"

"Yes," she admitted, "it is."

"You got family in the hospital?"

"My little brother."

"What's wrong with him? Is he hurt, sick, or what?"

"Hurt, I think."

The bus driver steered the bus around a corner, and Maggie leaned with the turn. She was the only passenger on the bus.

"Where's the rest of your family?"

"Well, my older brother and my grandfather are in city gaol."

"In gaol? You're putting me on."

"I wish I was."

"In gaol?"

"Yes, it's true."

"What'd they do?"

"I don't know exactly what Pap did. Vern went in on his own, through the vent."

"Your brother busted into gaol?"

"That's right. I helped him."

"*Into* gaol? Now you are jiving me."

"No, I'm not."

"And you helped him?"

"I gave him a boost."

"Man, this don't happen. People don't bust *into* gaol. Who-all knows he's in there?"

"Just Pap."

"The police don't know?"

"Nope."

"Whoeee, they'll have themselves a nice surprise in the morning. Be the first time anybody ever busted into gaol. I know some people like to bust out."

"Me too," said Maggie, thinking of Pap and Vern.

"Bust *into* gaol—that just don't happen. Whoa, bus. Look, I'm 'bout to go past your stop. There's Alderson General."

Maggie looked out of the window at the four-storey building. "Well, I thank you."

"You take care of yourself. You the only member of your family doing all right. Everybody else in gaol, in the hospital."

"I will."

Maggie felt rich and special. She decided it was a great combination. She got up and, holding her hand over the comforting wad of money in her pocket, got off the bus.

Junior was having the most wonderful, elegant dream of his life. He was in an orchestra, a huge orchestra, and he and all of the other musicians had on expensive black suits. The black suits were so expensive, they shone. They all—even the ladies—had on neckties.

In their hands were miniature silver musical instruments that really played. The instruments were the most beautiful things Junior had ever seen in his life.

The cymbals were the size of dimes. The piano was so small, the piano player had to poke the keys with toothpicks. The violins were one inch long; the bass fiddles, two inches. The orchestra leader had a baton like a straight pin.

Junior, of course, had his harmonica. He was

in the front row. He was standing up. He had his music on a silver stand. A spotlight shone on him.

He was wiping his harmonica daintily on the lapel of his black suit, getting the spit off for the second number, when a voice said, "Junior."

Junior did not open his eyes.

The orchestra leader was tapping his straight pin on his music stand. He lifted it in the air.

"Junior!"

The dream was too wonderful to lose. This was his one chance to be a star, to play in a real orchestra with chandeliers glowing and his black suit shining. This was the only time thousands of people in evening outfits would be smiling, waiting to clap for him. This was—

"Junior! It's me! Maggie!"

Junior opened his eyes.

Discoveries

The policeman who did the one o'clock check of the city gaol did not spot Vern. Vern was lying on the far side of Pap, against the wall, under the blanket, asleep. The two o'clock policeman didn't see him either; neither did the three and four o'clock policemen.

For three and a half hours Vern slept so soundly, he did not move one single time. Pap slept the same way. They might as well have been logs.

At four-thirty Vern moved for the first time. He slung one foot out from under the blanket and it landed on Pap's arm. Pap never even felt it.

The five o'clock policeman came in eating a ham and fried egg sandwich. He had been on duty all night and he was tired.

He just gave a quick check of the cells on the left, taking in with one glance the fact that everybody was in his bunk asleep. He turned his head, did the same quick sweep on the right.

He was ready to go back to the desk when he noticed something weird in the last cell. What in the—Take a look at that!

The old man's foot was on his arm. How did he manage that?

The policeman walked closer, his ham and fried egg sandwich forgotten in his hand. The only explanation he could think of was that the old man was some sort of contortionist, like the Living Pretzel whom the policeman had once seen in a sideshow.

But wait! What in the—Would you take a look at that!

There was a leg attached to the foot. It was a small leg. Too small.

The officer had been a member of the police force for twenty years but he had never seen anything like this. He walked closer. He saw now that the leg went under the blanket where there was a large bump. Coming out of the top of the bump was a lot of rumpled sandy-coloured hair.

The officer unlocked the cell without making a sound. He entered. He pulled back the blanket so carefully, the sleepers never even felt it. He looked at Vern. He looked up at the open vent.

He closed his eyes, shook his head, and a half smile came over his face. *Well, we've had a gaolbreak*, he said to himself. He laid the blanket gently back over the sleeping boy.

He went to the sergeant's desk. He shook his head. "You ain't going to believe this," he said.

Mud was hungry, and it was the first time in his life he had ever had to worry about food. His diet had always been simple. Whatever Pap ate, he ate. If Pap ate pancakes with syrup on them, he ate pancakes with syrup on them. If Pap ate stew, he ate stew.

Mud was moving into the downtown section of the city now, and the houses were close together. There were no nice lawns, no side yards. There weren't any swimming-pools or fine shrubberies either.

At one of the houses Mud paused. He smelt something of interest—a fishy smell. He lifted his nose, trying to find out where the smell was coming from.

Mud was fond of fish. Sometimes when Pap caught a fish in the creek, he would put it in a bucket of creek water and let Mud recatch it.

It was like bobbing for apples. Mud would thrust his whole head into the water, scramble around till he felt the fish in his mouth. Then he would come up.

Pap's laugh was Mud's reward, that and a piece of fried fish later. Mud held these fish in his mouth so gently, there was never a tooth mark on them.

Mud crossed the street. The smell seemed to be coming from this house . . . from this porch. Mud went up the steps. From this dish on this railing. Mud stood up and looked into the dish.

Mud was a good stander. He could even take a few steps on his hind legs when it was necessary. Mostly he stood up so he could get a better look at something.

It worked. Mud could see that the dish contained a ring of dark food, sort of smashed down into the bottom. He propped one foot on the banister and took the dish in his teeth. He set it down on the floor without a sound.

Mud took one small bite of the fish stuff. The taste was nothing like Pap's fish, and he stood looking at the dish with his brow drawn into wrinkles. He took a second bite.

This was the worst food Mud had ever had in his entire life. It was barely edible. If he hadn't been absolutely starved . . .

Mud finished the cat food, went down the steps, and was once again on his way through the dark streets of Alderson.

Ralphie opened his eyes and saw Maggie sitting cross-legged on the foot of Junior's bed. Her green eyes were shining; one of her braids lay on her tanned shoulder, she was chewing on the other in her excitement. Her cheeks were pink. She was grinning. She had one jagged tooth.

Even if she had not been telling the story of how she and Vern had bust into gaol, Ralphie would have fallen in love with her. His heart was pumping hard, like the machines he'd seen occasionally through the doors of Intensive Care.

"You busted into gaol?" Ralphie asked. He worked his way up in bed until he was sitting. He hadn't even bothered to push the control and bring the head of the bed up with him.

Maggie had learned from the bus driver the shock value of her story. Already it was her favourite story in the world. She loved to tell it. Her eyes got brighter.

"It was the only thing we could do. We had to."

"They had to," Junior echoed in the same delighted voice. He held out his empty hands to show there was no alternative.

"Pardon me for being nosy," Ralphie said, "but why didn't you just go in the police station and ask to see your grandfather?"

Maggie looked at him as if he were crazy. He wished he hadn't spoken. The tips of his ears turned red.

"Anybody could have done that," she said.

"Yes, anybody," piped Junior happily.

"We Blossoms," Maggie said proudly, "have never been just 'anybody'."

Ralphie believed her. For the first time in his life he had nothing to say.

Fame

BOY BREAKS INTO CITY GAOL was the headline. The story took up two columns on the front page.

BULLETIN:
Last night a local juvenile broke into city gaol by way of an old air vent. Using a board, which he placed in an elm tree beside the gaol, he crossed to the vent. The size of the vent was approximately seven inches by fourteen inches.

According to police, the boy entered city gaol just before midnight and slept in the cell with his grandfather, Alexander "Pap" Blossom, Sr., who is in gaol awaiting a hearing on a charge of maliciously disturbing the peace.

Officer Canfield, the policeman who found the boy during his five o'clock rounds, admitted that it had been quite a surprise. "I knew soon as I saw him that he wasn't supposed to be there. I went out and got the sergeant and took him in, and the sergeant was surprised too. He shook both the boy and the grandfather awake to find out what was going on."

When awakened, the grandfather asked one question, "What's wrong?" The officer admitted that the boy was still in his grandfather's cell but would be moved, he said, "as soon as we figure out what to do with him.

109

"We let him out for breakfast, but he wanted to go right back in afterwards, so we let him. We're taking it one hour at a time."

The grandfather's hearing is scheduled for this afternoon.

There was a large picture of Pap and Vern sitting on the bunk, side by side. Their hands were on their knees, their heads turned stiffly to the photographer. It was like a photograph taken fifty years ago.

Neither one of them looked scared, unhappy, or regretful.

Under the picture was the caption: "Local policeman caught off guard by unique gaolbreak."

"Hey, you weren't kidding!" Ralphie said.

Ralphie had been walking up and down the hall on his new leg, mainly in the hope of impressing Maggie. At the desk he had seen the morning newspaper.

"I want to borrow this," he said.

He hurried back to the room, hopping spryly on his new leg. "There." He threw the paper, headline up, on Junior's bed.

"That's them!" Junior cried, drawing in his breath. "They're famous!"

"Give me that," Maggie said.

"What does it say?"

"This is what it says." Maggie snapped the newspaper open. She read the story aloud, stum-

110

bling only on the words *juvenile* and *maliciously*.
When she was through, she held the paper at
arm's length and looked at the picture critically.

Then she said, "That doesn't look a thing like
Vern, does it, Junior?"

"Not a thing." Junior was so glad to have
Maggie with him that he had become her echo.

"And they made Pap look like an old bum."

"A real old bum," Junior said.

Ralphie said, "Reporters try to take unflatter-
ing pictures. That's part of their training. They
throw the good pictures in the trash can."

For the first time Maggie looked at him with
interest.

"He tells lies," Junior said quickly, seeing
Maggie's look. He did not want to share Maggie
with anybody. "He told me he had water-melon
seeds inside him and marbles in his head."

Ralphie's ears turned red.

"Maybe he lied about that," Maggie admitted.
She was beginning to like the boy with the
artificial leg. "But he sure tells the truth about
reporters."

"Maybe," Junior conceded.

Ralphie was so pleased with Maggie's compli-
ment that he hopped around the room on his
artificial leg.

"Stop that, Ralphie!" the nurse called from the
door. "You're supposed to walk on the leg, not
jump on it. You're going to bust those stitches."

"It doesn't hurt at all," Ralphie said, lying.

111

Trucks and Cabs and 1-85

Mud did not know what to do about the Interstate. The only time he had been on 1-85 before, he had been sitting beside Pap in the cab of the pick-up, with wind that smelt of exhaust fumes whipping his ears back from his face.

He had come to 1-85 today at the peak of the midday traffic. He had turned down the exit ramp because the air in that direction smelt more familiar than the air in any other direction. Now he faced more traffic than he had ever seen in his life.

He waited and watched. He knew he had to get across it—the air told him that—but he didn't know how. The traffic was solid—a double line of trucks and cars and buses and vans, all exceeding the speed limit.

He walked nervously back and forth, pacing, his eyes on the steady stream of traffic coming through the underpass. He breathed air thick with exhaust fumes. He blinked every time a truck threw gravel in his direction.

Mud's tongue was hanging out. His throat was dry. He had not had a drop of water for three hours, not since the cat-food snack. And the cat-food snack had left him thirsty.

An hour ago he had come across a dust hole. With Mud, there was nothing to do with a dust hole but get in it and roll around. Mud preferred the back method. He lay on his back and twisted from side to side. His eyes closed in bliss, he moaned with pleasure.

Afterwards, refreshed, he got up and shook himself. A red cloud grew around him.

As he left the dust hole he felt better but looked worse. To see him loping along the side of the road, a person would think Mud had never had a bath in his life. The bandanna around his neck looked like a dust rag.

A small break came in the right lane. Mud started out, then darted back as a truck roared down the fast lane at seventy-five miles an hour. Mud crouched on the grass while fine gravel rained around him. He fell back to wait for another chance.

He was going to get across 1-85 if it killed him.

"Well, I better be on my way," Maggie said with studied casualness.

Maggie had been in the hospital for twelve hours, and she could not have been happier if she had been in the ritziest hotel in New York City. Everything she wanted, or would ever want, was right here.

She had just finished lunch. She had bought a pimento cheese sandwich from a vending machine, heated it miraculously in a small oven, and washed it down with an ice-cold Mello-Yello.

Before that she had napped in the waiting room, on a long plastic sofa, while watching *Let's Make a Deal*. She got to see a man dressed like a hot dog win a Westinghouse refrigerator. This was living.

"Be on your way?" This was the worst news Ralphie had ever heard in his life. He was at her side in an instant. "Where are you going?"

Maggie yawned. "To the court-house, of course. My grandfather's hearing is this afternoon."

"You're going to the hearing?" Junior wailed.

Junior was in a wheelchair for the first time, his legs propped in front of him. He rolled himself forward a few inches. "I want to go too."

"You can't."

"I have to!"

"No."

"I *have* to!"

Junior could not bear to be left again. He had not even started to recover from being left on the roof. That was the worst thing that had happened to him, worse even than the broken legs. Breaking legs he could stand; being left he couldn't.

"I'm sorry, Junior, I would never be able to get you on the bus," Maggie said sensibly. "I rode the bus last night and there was not a single wheelchair person on it. There are no ramps, no—"

"You can get me on. Please! I promise you can get me on," Junior wailed.

"Junior, you have two broken legs. You're in a wheelchair!"

"I'll walk if you get me crutches. I promise I'll walk. Please!" He would have gone down on his knees if he had been able to bend.

"No."

"Then I'll get my own crutches."

Junior propelled himself towards the door, but this was his first time in the wheelchair. The chair swerved into the foot of his bed.

Junior hung his head in defeat. He began to cry. "I want to go! I want to go!"

Maggie was softened by his tears. "I'll tell you all about it when I get back. I'll remember every single thing that happens. It'll be just like being there."

Junior shook his head from side to side in a fit of rage and frustration too terrible to be expressed in any other way. "No! No! No! No—"

It was Ralphie who stopped the explosion of *no's*. He took one step forward on his artificial leg.

"We," he said. There was something in his quiet, take-charge voice that made Junior stop crying and look up. "We could take a cab," Ralphie said.

Maggie looked at him and her face lit up with Junior's. At that moment they looked like brother and sister.

Maggie threw her braids behind her back and grinned, showing her jagged tooth. "Why didn't I think of that?" she said. "Of course! We'll take a cab."

115

Going to Court

"Gentleman to see you," the policeman told Pap.

Pap threw up his hands to protect himself. "No more reporters. I'm not talking to no more reporters." His old head wagged tiredly from side to side, begging for mercy.

"Me neither," said Vern, who was sitting beside him.

"This is not a reporter. It's a lawyer."

Pap's head snapped up. "Lawyer?"

"The best the town's got—Henry Ward Bowman."

"What's he want with me?"

"He says he wants to defend you."

"For how much?" Pap asked suspiciously.

"For free."

Now Pap was even more suspicious. "Why?"

"You want my opinion?"

Pap nodded reluctantly. He hated to ask a policeman for anything.

"Mr Bowman's getting ready to make a run for the State Senate, and I imagine he thinks it wouldn't do him any harm to get you off and get himself some publicity doing it. You may not know this, but we've had more calls about you and the boy than about anything else that's ever happened in the police department, even the Safeway robbery last year. People don't like to see a grandfather being arrested for nothing more than defending a load of pop cans from some reckless teenagers. People don't like to see a boy forced to bust into gaol to be with him."

Pap watched the policeman with sharp eyes, taking in every word.

The policeman shrugged. "That's how the public sees this whole thing anyway."

That was how Pap saw it, too. He started stage one of getting to his feet—the crouch. Then he rose to his full height of six feet.

He tucked his shirt-tail into his pants. He fished in his hip pocket for a comb. He raked it through his tangled hair, then he swept the sides back like wings, the way he did on special occasions.

He slapped the comb against his palm to clear it of stray hairs. Then he slid it back in his pocket.

"Show Mr Bowman in," he said.

It was two o'clock in the afternoon, and Mud had started barking at the traffic. He had been trying to cross 1-85 for thirty-five minutes, and the traffic wouldn't let him.

Mud was tired, sore of foot, thirsty, and desperate. Most of all, he wanted Pap.

At two-ten someone threw a can out of a car window. It struck the concrete beside Mud and bounced into his side. Startled, Mud shied away, almost backing into traffic coming down the ramp.

It seemed to Mud then that he was surrounded by danger. There was no safety anywhere. In a panic he headed for the Interstate.

The right lane was clear. A semi was barrelling down the fast lane.

Ears back, tail down, Mud ran.

"I'll do that," Ralphie said. He took Junior's wheelchair, unlocked two springs underneath, folded it in half, and snapped it shut with practised skill.

Junior was in the back seat of the yellow cab with his legs resting on Maggie's lap. Ralphie put the folded wheelchair in the front seat and squeezed in beside it.

"Court-house, please," he told the driver.

The driver nodded, and the cab moved out from under the hospital awning.

"Good-bye, Hospital," Junior called with a happy wave.

The cab made the turn on to Main Street. It began to pick up speed.

Maggie spent the first few minutes of the cab ride admiring Ralphie. For those few minutes she watched the back of his shaggy head and returned his love wholeheartedly.

Ralphie was a man of the world, the first Maggie had known. She remembered with admiration the quick, assured way he had manœvred them out of the hospital. It had been like something out of a movie.

"Hold the elevator, please," he had called. Someone held it.

Ralphie swirled Junior's chair around and guided it in the elevator backwards. "Thank you," he said in the same tone of voice Maggie heard hospital workers use. "Everyone going to the lobby?" he asked, pushing the L button.

The nurse at the desk yelled, "Where are you taking Junior, Ralphie?"

"Gift shop," Ralphie called back cheerfully as the doors began to close.

"Bring him back this—"

The word was cut off, but inside the elevator Ralphie supplied it with a smile: "—instant."

Everyone in the elevator laughed, and they were swept down to the lobby. It was like a miracle. Maggie kept taking sideways glances at Ralphie. He kept his eyes on the elevator doors.

"Coming through," Ralphie called as they came out of the elevator. People in the lobby made way for them.

"Cab!"

And the cab pulled up in front of the hospital. It was as if the cab had been waiting just for them. This was the way things went for celebrities, Maggie thought: instant service.

"Court-house, please." Ralphie said it as if he went daily to the court-house.

Maggie sighed with pleasure. She was beginning to appreciate people who knew how to handle themselves in this increasingly complex world.

She leaned back and admired the way the city of Alderson looked through the window of a yellow cab.

Order in the Court

The story of Vern's gaolbreak was picked up by every newspaper in the country, and the picture of Vern and Pap was on every front page, including the front page of *The Pecos Daily News and World Report* of Pecos, Texas.

Vicki Blossom was coming out of the TexiMex Motel with two girlfriends she was sharing a room with. Another friend was waiting for them. This friend was leaning against the fender of the pick-up truck they were driving to the rodeo; she was reading the newspaper.

"Hey, Vicki," she called, folding the newspaper against her so the front page was hidden, "isn't Pap Blossom your daddy-in-law?"

"Yes."

"Does he still live in—" she opened the paper and checked the name of the town, "—Alderson?"

"Last I heard," Vicki said cheerfully. She was swinging her hat in the air.

"And have you got a little boy about ten or eleven?"

"Vern's eleven, Junior's seven." She stopped swinging her hat.

"Have you talked to them lately?"

"The lady at the motel said Vern called about

121

four days ago—this was when we were at the Paisano—but the only message was that everything at home was all right. I didn't get to talk to him because I was sharing a room with you guys and my name wasn't on the register." She came forward with her hat in both hands. "Why?"

When her friend was slow in answering, Vicki said again, sharply this time, "Why?"

"Because according to this newspaper everything is not so all right."

"What? Let me see. Gimme."

Vicki Blossom took the newspaper with hands that had started to tremble. "Oh, my Lord," she said, "look at that. My daddy-in-law and my oldest boy are in gaol."

She started back into the TexiMex Motel reading the little print. "Go on without me," she told her friends. "I'm going home."

The courtroom was packed. Twelve reporters from state newspapers and representatives from NBC, CBS and ABC were there with cameras. Both David Hartley and Bryant Gumbel had expressed an interest in interviews.

There were also 347 interested citizens who were trying to get into the courtroom for the hearing. Some of them had been interviewed by the reporters, and they all agreed that Pap should go free.

Pap, Mr Bowman, Vern, and the two cardplayers who were defending drunk and disorderly charges sat in the front row. Pap had on a clean shirt and pressed trousers which the lawyer had provided. Vern's hair had been wet and combed down flat. They both looked honest, respectable, and miserable. They couldn't wait to get out of court and look like themselves again.

The judge rapped his gavel.

The room got quiet. The bailiff announced that the Blossom case would be heard first. "Yes, there seems to be an unusual amount of interest in this matter," the judge said.

Pap got up in a stoop, rose, and followed his lawyer to the table. "You may be seated." They sat.

The judge told the lawyer prosecuting the case to begin. "I'd first like to call Officer Mahon," he said.

Officer Mahon was sworn in and the prosecutor asked him to describe what occurred on the afternoon Pap was arrested.

"Well, sir, we got a call about three-thirty Monday afternoon to go to Spring Street. The call came in from a citizen who reported a man with a gun had threatened some pedestrians. Also that the street was unusable, being completely clogged with beer and pop cans."

"What did you do after you got this information?"

"We went to the scene."

"And what did you observe?"

"We observed Mr Blossom there on Spring Street with a weapon."

123

"Did you determine what kind of weapon it was and whether or not it was loaded?"

"Yes, sir. It was a single barrel shotgun and I could tell by the temperature of the barrel and the powder marks near the hammer that it had been recently discharged. From the evidence at the scene and based on my past experience, I could tell that a traffic light had been hit by a shotgun discharge."

"After you made these observations what did you do?"

"I arrested Mr Blossom."

"What was his attitude at the time of his arrest?"

"Mr Blossom appeared confused as to the reason for his arrest. He did not think he had done anything wrong. We put handcuffs on him and got him into the patrol car. After that, he never said a word or gave us any trouble."

"Thank you, Officer Mahon."

Mud was on the median strip of 1-85. He had managed to cross the southbound double lane, and now faced the northbound. He had intended to run straight across both of them, but there had been some nice pine trees planted in the median strip, and Mud was so exhausted he lay down under the low branches.

He closed his eyes. A flea crawled in the dusty fur behind his ear. He was too tired to scratch. The steady drone of traffic seemed far away.

Without opening his eyes he settled his body

into a more comfortable spot in the pine needles and fell asleep.

Mr Bowman was on his feet. He was an inch taller than Abraham Lincoln, and he had the same kind of old-timey eyeglasses. He looked around the courtroom over the top of them.

The judge said, "Mr Bowman, it's a little unusual to see you taking an interest in this county's criminal court."

"I know, your honour, but my interest in justice is not limited to civil matters."

"Well, we're pleased to have you in court today. You may proceed."

"Thank you, your honour. I'd like to begin by calling Pap Blossom."

Pap got up in a stoop, rose, and took the stand.

The Rest of the Blossoms

The yellow cab pulled up in front of the courthouse. In the back seat Maggie had taken out her package of money and was unwrapping it carefully, preparing to count out the $4.65 cab fare.

"I'll get it," Ralphie said casually, as if he paid for cabs every day of his life.

"Why, thank you." Maggie folded up her money.

"It's nothing," Ralphie said. Then he surprised himself by adding something he had heard only on television: "Keep the change."

Actually he was extremely relieved that he had had enough money. If his mother had not left him five dollars to pay for his TV rental, he wouldn't have.

Ralphie got out of the cab and skilfully unfolded the wheelchair. Maggie and the cab driver helped Junior get in.

Junior was so excited over going to court and being in a wheelchair that he couldn't stop grinning. He kept closing his lips over his teeth because he knew it wouldn't be proper to grin in a criminal court, but he couldn't help himself. He didn't want to grin, but his lips did.

He glanced at Maggie to see if she was giving him a disapproving look. It made him feel a little better to see that Maggie was smiling too.

"Let me push him up the ramp for you," the cab driver said.

"Thanks," Ralphie said quickly.

Now that the money crisis was over, Ralphie had started worrying that he wouldn't be able to push Junior up the ramp without asking for help. His own leg hurt so bad, he wouldn't have minded having a wheelchair himself.

"Be careful with him," Maggie said.

"Don't worry. I was in a wheelchair myself for a year after the war."

A reporter who had arrived too late to get into the crowded courtroom was sitting on the courthouse steps. He watched their slow progress up the ramp. There had to be a story in these people.

The reporter got up. He said hopefully, "Do you three have anything to do with the man who got arrested and the boy that broke into gaol?"

"We sure do," Maggie said. "The boy is our brother, and the man is our grandfather."

The man took their picture twice. He already had his caption: "Blossom family arrives at the court-house."

"Wait, let me help you inside. I'll take them the rest of the way," he told the cab driver.

They went through the double doors and made their way down the hall. The doors to the courtroom had been left open so that the overflow crowd could hear the case.

"Could we get through, please," the reporter asked. "This is the rest of the Blossom family."

Ralphie did not bother to mention that he was just a friend. He was honoured to have been mistaken for a Blossom. He crowded through behind the wheelchair.

It was four o'clock and Mud awoke. He was rested. He lay for a moment without moving, his bright golden eyes watching the traffic below him on 1-85.

He got up. He discovered with pleasure that the lowest branch of the pine tree was just over the part of his back that always itched. He moved back and forth, back and forth, scratching the spot on the convenient pine branch. He closed his eyes, blocking out the traffic and the noise in the pleasure of scratching the spot that only he and Pap knew about.

Pap was always good about scratching Mud with his shoe. Mud would see Pap's foot dangling at just the right height, and he would go over and stand under it. Pap never failed to move his foot exactly where it itched.

The pine branch was a good substitute, though. The loose bark rained around him.

When Mud's itch was satisfied, he moved out from under the pine tree. The traffic had thinned, but Mud wasn't thinking about that. Mud had just smelt water, and Mud was very thirsty.

He moved to the right, nose up. The smell seemed to be this way. He went over the slight hill that bulldozers had created between the highways. The grass was soft and had just been mowed.

Mud skirted another stand of pine trees. The smell of water was stronger. He turned his nose down like a divining rod.

In a deep grassy ditch a small stream of water trickled into a drainage pipe. Mud's eyes shone, and he bounded down the slope.

He drank lustily, his rough tongue brushing against the corrugated pipe. He had never tasted better water in his life, not even from the family toilet.

He drank, and when that little puddle of water was gone, he moved deeper into the pipe. Another small pool of water between those ridges. Mud drank. He moved deeper into the pipe, drinking between each ridge, enjoying it more because it was cool and scarce.

Mud moved through the pipe in a stoop, drinking as he went. There was not a sound of the traffic overhead until he came out the other side. Then he heard it—the cars and trucks behind him.

The air smelt familiar this way, so he ran up the embankment. There was a chain-link fence there, blocking his way. Mud didn't hesitate. Mud knew what to do about fences.

Mud began to dig.

The Verdict

Maggie, Ralphie, and Junior got through the crowd at the back of the courtroom. The first thing they saw was Pap walking back to the table with his head down. His face was as red as a beet.

Pap was in misery. His head was pounding. His throat was dry. He took out his worn handkerchief and wiped the sweat from his face. His hands were trembling.

It wasn't the fear of going to gaol that was making him miserable. He'd been in gaol and it wasn't so bad. It wasn't the fact that he could be fined five hundred dollars. A man couldn't pay what he didn't have.

It was being questioned. Pap had never been able to abide people asking him questions. Nobody in his family could. It was a family trait.

And here he had to sit as if he were in chains, and let anybody ask him anything they wanted to—the prosecutor, the judge, and Henry Ward Bowman, who was trying to act like Lincoln.

A dozen times he had wanted to interrupt and say, "Just send me to gaol and get it over with." It would have been a relief to be led back to his corner cell.

The only thing that stopped him was that out of the corner of his eye he could see Vern's feet, Vern's worn tennis shoes. Above all, Pap didn't want to make Vern's gaolbreak seem like it had been in vain.

"In conclusion, your honour," Mr Bowman was saying, "Mr Blossom has had an absolutely clean record. He has a high and respected reputation in this community. He has never been arrested; he has never had a traffic ticket; and it is only through the series of unusual and bewildering events which he testified about this afternoon that we are even here today. Mr Blossom is not a criminal and he should not be found guilty of a criminal offence."

Pap was so lost in misery that the judge had to rap his gavel on the desk three times to get his attention.

"Mr Blossom!"

Pap looked up.

"I said I have reached a decision in your case."

The laywer helped Pap to his feet.

"Mr Blossom, I agree with your lawyer that the events of Monday were to a large extent the result of a chain of unfortunate incidents. However, it is my duty to protect the lives of the people of this country. We cannot allow citizens to take the law into their own hands."

Pap nodded.

"I find you guilty on the charge of disturbing the peace and sentence you to sixty days in county gaol."

Pap nodded. He turned and headed for the door, where the policeman waited to take him back to his cell.

"However—"

The lawyer stopped Pap and turned him around.

"However, because of the circumstances and because you obviously have the wholehearted love of at least one member of your family," the judge nodded at Vern, "I'm suspending your sentence on the condition that I do not see you in this court again."

Pap nodded.

"Mr Blossom, you may go now."

Pap stood blinking in the courtroom. He spoke willingly for the first time since he had entered the courtroom. "Home?" he asked in a bewildered, incredulous way.

"Yes, Mr Blossom, you are free to go home."

Mud was a good digger. He never dug around the farm unless it was a gopher or snake hole and Pap indicated it was all right to dig. Pap would do this by pointing with the toe of one worn shoe at the hole. "What's that, Mud?" Pap would ask. "What's down there?"

Mud would dive in. He would dig so hard the dirt would fly over his back. He never actually got his teeth on a gopher or snake, but he sure was a good digger.

It took Mud seventeen minutes to dig the hole halfway under the fence. Then he had to dig the rest of the way on his side, working his lean body under the chain, pushing the dirt behind him with his paws.

He squirmed out on the other side and immediately began shaking the clay from his fur. He still felt dirty. There was a patch of grass by the trees and Mud rolled in that. Then he shook himself again.

Satisfied, he started through the woods.

Maggie cried, "Pap!"

She pushed Junior down the aisle and to the front of the court-house so fast, Junior screamed. He thought his legs were going to ram all the way through the judge's desk. The judge rapped his gavel.

"It's us!" she cried.

In bewilderment Pap watched her come. Maggie let go of the wheelchair to throw her arms around him, then around the startled Vern. She had never embraced either one of them before.

Junior's chair did a wheelie which left him facing the room and the reporters. Cameras clicked.

The judge rapped again for order.

"Perhaps," the judge said, "the Blossom family could continue this family reunion in my chambers."

"That's very kind, your honour," the lawyer said. As the cameras rolled, he ushered them all towards the chamber door, imagining how fine this would look on the evening news.

At the door Maggie turned and beckoned to Ralphie. "This includes you," she said.

Going Home

Ralphie and Junior were on their way back to the hospital in a police car. Neither one of them had put up a fuss. They were glad to go. Both of them wanted to get back in bed. Their legs hurt.

"I'll come see you," Maggie had said to Junior. She leaned down and looked into the car so she could see Ralphie too. "I'll come see both of you."

She grinned, showing her chipped tooth, and threw her braids behind her shoulders. Then she closed the car door.

"Good-bye," Junior said. Then, after a pause, he added, "Maggie," so she would know he was speaking to her instead of the court-house.

For the first time in his life he was not saying good-bye to a building, even though this afternoon the court-house had become Junior's all-time favourite building in the world. He really loved the court-house. He loved his family more.

"Good-bye, Pap!" He called through the glass. "Good-bye, Vern!"

Vern and Pap didn't hear him. They were on the steps of the court-house having their pictures taken. Both Pap and Vern would have been long gone except that the lawyer had an arm around each of them and was bodily holding them in place. Their arms were clamped straight down at their sides.

Reporters were calling out questions as if it were a news conference. Vern's questions were: "Son, tell us how you decided to break into gaol? How did you feel when you got inside? Were you scared? Would you do it again? Have you got anything to say about security at city gaol?"

Pap's questions were: "Sir, how did you feel when you saw your grandson coming through the vent? What are your plans now that you're free? What did the boy's mother say when she heard he was in gaol? Do you ever plan to collect any more pop cans?"

Neither Pap nor Vern said a word. The lawyer did the talking. Finally, when he'd had all the attention he was likely to get, he lifted his hands. Pap and Vern started down the steps. The reporters followed.

"Now, you guys give these folks a break. They've been through a lot. I'll tell you exactly what we're going to do. First, we're going to ride over and get Mr Blossom's truck, and then he and his grandchildren are going home. I am, too."

With a laugh, Henry Ward Bowman guided Pap and Vern to his car. He got in the front. Vern and Pap and Maggie squeezed in the back. Mr Bowman and Maggie waved for the cameras. Vern and Pap did not.

*

It was dusk and Mud stopped to lick his foot. It hurt. His tongue found a sharp point that wasn't supposed to be there. Something had stuck into his foot, between the pads, a thorn of some kind.

Mud tried to take the stub in his teeth. It was too short. He dug into the flesh of his foot so deeply, his nose wrinkled. It hurt a lot, but this time he got the end of the thorn.

Mud pulled it out and spat it on the ground. He looked at it closely before he went back to licking his sore paw.

Mud was so intent on his sore paw that he failed to hear a noise behind him. He kept licking.

A skunk stuck his head out of the hollow tree behind Mud. The skunk couldn't see Mud because of the ferns. Mud hadn't seen the skunk for the same reason, and Mud had not smelt the skunk because the skunk was downwind.

The skunk was beginning his evening search for food. It was beetle and bug season, and they were all fat, crisp, and oily. Next month there would be crickets and grasshoppers and, after that, caterpillars. The skunk was hungry.

The skunk came through the ferns, as he always did. His nose was to the ground. His tail was relaxed.

Mud got up. Now he heard the noise behind him. Ferns rustled; parted. He swirled around. The hair rose on his back.

Too late he saw the long pointed nose, the

black and white fur. Too late he recognized the smell.

Mud's tail dropped between his legs at the same moment that the skunk swirled, flared, thumped his hind legs on the ground, and sent a stream of liquid in Mud's direction.

In an instant Mud was blinded. He ran yelping with pain and fear around the small clearing. He ran into trees and briars, senselessly trying to run away from the pain and the fear and the blindness, and getting nowhere.

Skirting the yelping, panic-stricken dog, the skunk proceeded on his evening rounds. He found a beetle under the first stone he overturned.

"Drop me off at the emergency entrance," Ralphie told the policeman as they turned into the hospital.

"Me, too," Junior said. If he could help it, he would never be separated from Ralphie again.

Ralphie turned to him. "We can pick up another wheelchair for me and a couple of interns and get pushed up to our room."

"Good," Junior said.

"We'll probably be there in time for supper."

"Good." Suddenly Junior had his first unpleasant thought of the afternoon. "Maybe," he said in a rush, "they really will put medicine in our food now. Maybe because we ran away, they'll want us to be so groggy we can't do it again."

"Nah," said Ralphie. "They wouldn't dare."

Mud's Missing

"Where's my dog?"

"What?"

"The dog that was in the truck. Where's my dog?"

This was the first time Pap had ever worried about Mud. He had never had to before because Mud was the most sensible member of the Blossom family. He knew what he was supposed to do, and he did it. It was as simple as that.

Pap had not doubted for a minute that Mud would be with the truck, in the back, curled up on his gunny-sack. Either that or he would be nearby getting something to eat or drink.

When he saw the man's blank look, he let out a piercing whistle that went up and down like a siren. It would be heard for a mile.

"I don't know anything about any dog," the man at the garage said, stepping back out of Pap's reach.

"Who towed Mr Blossom's truck in?" the lawyer asked.

"When was this?"

"Monday."

"Pete was working Monday, I believe. Arnie, ask Pete if he knows anything about this man's dog."

The Blossoms waited in silence by the truck. Maggie had become so used to things getting better that tears of disappointment filled her eyes. It had seemed like the whole rest of her life was going to be like that—better and better and better. Now, after just one day of getting better, it was getting worse again.

And she had not given one single thought to Mud! She whisked the tears away with the tips of her braids.

Pete came out of the garage wiping oil off his hands. "I never seen any dog," he said.

"He was a tall dog," Vern said, "with gold-coloured eyes and a red bandanna around his neck. His name was Mud."

"I never seen a dog of any description."

Pap touched one finger to his forehead, trying to remember whether Mud had got out of the truck at the scene of the accident. If he had, Mud would most likely be there, on Spring Street, waiting. He gave another whistle just in case.

"You could put an ad in the paper," Mr Bowman said. "Or, better still, let the newspaper do a story for you. Your family is news now, Mr Blossom. Call the paper and tell them about your dog—what was his name?"

"Mud."

"I'll call them for you and ask them to send a reporter to the farm. Somebody in town will have seen the dog."

The Blossoms kept standing around. None of

them wanted to leave, because it would be like giving up on Mud.

Pete said helpfully, "Your truck's running good. We tuned her up and took care of the expired inspection sticker. Mr Bowman took care of the licence. You're ready to roll."

Still the Blossoms stood there.

Finally Vern said, "Pap, maybe we ought to go. Maybe Mud's waiting downtown."

"That's what I'm hoping," Pap said.

He led the way to the truck and they got in. "You folks have a nice day," Pete called after them.

Ralphie's mother was waiting for Ralphie in the hospital room. The minute she saw him she leapt up from her chair. She had come to the hospital in such a rush that she had on a dress over her bathing suit.

Ralphie said, "Hi, Mom. What are you doing here?"

Ralphie's mom said, "Don't you 'hi' me, and I'll tell you exactly what I'm doing here."

Ralphie's mom said, "Ralphie, the nurse called me on the phone and told me what you did. I cannot believe that you would take this little boy with two broken legs in a cab to the court-house. Do you realize that you could have done permanent injury to this little boy? The nurse said today was the first time he had even got up. One of his legs is broken in two places. If you have done any damage to either one of that little boy's legs, your dad's going to wear you out."

Ralphie's mom turned to Junior. "Are you all right? I am just so sorry for what my son did. I apologise for him."

"He didn't do me any damage," Junior said. "I enjoyed it."

Pap hated to return to the scene of the accident. As soon as he turned the corner on to Spring Street, it all came back to him—the abrupt stop, the falling cans, the boys in the Toyota, the police attack.

"Right here's where it happened," he told Vern and Maggie in a low, sad voice.

There was a parking slot in front of Woolco, and Pap backed into it.

The three of them got out. Pap let out a piercing whistle. Everybody on the block turned around to find out where the noise had come from, but Mud did not come bounding into view with his ears flying, eyes shining, as they had hoped.

"Maybe he's around the back," Vern said, "where they throw the garbage. Maybe he's back there eating out of the dumpster."

"Go see."

Maggie and Pap waited, without speaking, for Vern to come back. Their hope died as they heard him calling "Mud! Mu-ud! Mud!" from the back of the Winn Dixie.

Vern came around the store shaking his head.

142

"Not there?"

"No."

"Well," Pap said. "That's that." He sighed so deeply that he seemed to get shorter. "Well, there's nothing to do but go home."

'There's still the reporters," Maggie said. "I know they'll be able to find him. I *know* they will."

"Maybe," Pap said. He swallowed, almost choking on his next words because he hated reporters so much. "If they do, I'll be mighty grateful."

The three of them climbed into the truck. As they drove off, Maggie said. "You look on that side of the road, Vern, and I'll look on this side. Maybe we'll see him."

They watched all the way home, but neither of them did.

In the News

A description of Mud appeared in the state paper along with a story about the trial. The head-line was BLOSSOM DOG LOST FOLLOWING OWNER'S ARREST.

BULLETIN:
Yesterday, following the release of Pap Blossom, it was learned that his dog, Mud, had been frightened during his owner's arrest and had run away. Several people reported seeing a dog fitting Mud's description running through the downtown area.

Later Mud was spotted at a local Dairy Queen, lying beneath the carryout window. He appeared to be in a coma, one woman said. Several people offered him bits of food, but he would not eat. When the Dairy Queen opened the next day, the dog was gone.

The dog has not been seen since, although there have been various unconfirmed reports of a dog seen on 1-85 yesterday afternoon.

Mud is a large dog with short, yellowish fur. He has golden eyes. He has a piece of an old red bandanna tied around his neck.

Anyone seeing a dog answering this description is asked to call the police department. Mr

144

Henry Ward Bowman, Pap Blossom's lawyer, has offered a fifty-dollar reward.

Beside the story, in the centre column, was a police artist's composite drawing of Mud. Mud had never had his picture taken, so this was the best they could do.

Vern, Maggie and Pap had been satisfied with the likeness.

"That's him," Pap said.

"Yes, that's exactly the way he looks," Maggie had said, "when he's feeling—" tears filled her eyes, "—when he's feeling happy."

Vicki Blossom stopped for a hamburger at a diner just across the state line. She saw Mud's face looking at her through the newspaper dispenser. She got out a quarter as quickly as she could.

She went into the diner reading.

"Well, what next?" she asked the man on the stool next to hers. She showed him the front page. "My daddy-in-law was arrested, my little boy busted into gaol to get him out, and now there's an all-points bulletin for our dog."

"I hear the old man got off."

She nodded. "That's what they tell me. I've been calling the police and the hospital and the lawyer. I can't get anybody. I'll be home this afternoon to see things for myself."

She ordered a hamburger and settled down to read the story.

"Look," she said, "there's all my kids. My youngest boy is in the wheelchair, two broken legs, and he's grinning like it's Christmas.

"There's Maggie, my girl, and she's got better sense than to take her little brother out of the hospital. She practically kidnapped him, according to the nurse. I don't know who this boy is. That's probably the cab driver."

She looked closely at the third picture. "This— I almost didn't recognize him with his hair combed—is my daddy-in-law, and this is my oldest boy, Vern. This man between them is the lawyer."

She drank some coffee to get the strength to look at the newspaper some more. She shook her head.

"I can't believe this. My whole family smeared across the front page of the state paper. I'm going to have to straighten every one of them out."

Ralphie said, "Well, good-bye."

"I wish you didn't have to go."

"I do, though. You heard my mom."

Junior nodded.

"You and everybody else in the hospital," Ralphie added.

Ralphie's mom had come to take him home that morning. She was still mad. She said, "If you can get around that good, good enough to tramp downtown to the court-house, you can get around good enough to go home."

"I've got to have my therapy!" Ralphie had cried. "You want me to be a cripple?"

She pointed at him. "You"—it was like something Junior had seen once on a poster—"are going home."

"Well, can I at least put my leg on?"

She was already storming down the hall. She did not answer.

"You want me to read the story about Mud one more time before I go?"

Junior nodded. This would make the eighth time, but Junior would never get tired of hearing it.

"'Bulletin: Yesterday, following the release of Pap Blossom . . .'"

The Hero

The sight of his mom in the hospital doorway caused Junior to burst into tears.

She rushed to his bed. "Junior, let me look at you. I have been so worried. Darling, how are you?"

"I'm fine."

"No, you aren't. Let me see those legs." She threw back the sheet. "Both of them. You broke both of them." Tears came to her eyes, too.

He nodded.

"Well, one good thing about our family is that our bones heal fast. Your dad broke seventeen bones in his lifetime and never spent one day in the hospital. He took the casts off himself."

Junior's mom always knew how to make him feel better. He wiped his tears on the sleeve of his pyjamas. "Did they find Mud?"

The newspaper was still on his lap. He had shed so many tears on the composite drawing of Mud that the picture looked bubbly. Since Ralphie had gone, Junior had not had anyone to read the story to him, but he had looked at the pictures so much, he had them memorized.

The cheerful one of himself in his wheelchair was his favourite. He would feel better every time he looked at that one. Then he would see Mud, and tears would drop from his eyes. He was careful not to get any on his own picture.

"I don't know, Junior. I haven't been home. I drove straight to the hospital to see you. Sandy Boy's outside in his trailer."

"I went to the court-house."

"I know you did. I read about it in the newspaper."

"The boy that was in that bed took me, but he's gone home."

"Well, you'll be going home, too, now that I'm here to take care of you. I'm going right down to talk to the nurse."

"Talk to the big redheaded one," Junior called after her. "She's the nicest."

His mother disappeared around the door and started down the hall. There was a pause and then Junior sat straight up in bed.

"Get my harmonica!" he yelled.

"I keep hearing something. Do you?" Maggie said. "It sounds like Mud, but he's real far away."

"You *think* you hear something."

"No, I do."

"You *wish* you heard something." Vern corrected her because he wanted her to know he understood exactly how she felt. He had been hearing things himself. "Maybe it's thunder."

Maggie nodded. "Maybe." She dropped down beside him on the steps. "Mom's coming home this afternoon."

149

"I know it. I was standing right beside you when the policeman told us."

"I wish she'd hurry."

Maggie stretched out her legs. As usual she had on boy's clothes. She was older than Vern but smaller, so she got what he had outgrown. Today she had on a pair of his last summer's shorts and a shirt so old, it didn't have a button on it. Maggie had tied a knot in the shirt-tails to keep it closed.

After a long moment Maggie said, "You know, Vern, it wasn't a stupid idea after all."

"What?"

"Your idea. Busting into gaol."

Vern had come to that conclusion himself, but it was something he longed to hear about. "Why do you say that?" He shifted his feet and looked at Maggie out of the corners of his eyes.

"Well, because if you hadn't busted into gaol, Pap wouldn't have got off, and Mom wouldn't have seen the newspaper, and she wouldn't be coming home. Why, if you hadn't busted into gaol, we'd be right back where we were that night outside the gaol—desperate and helpless."

Vern swallowed. He closed his eyes as if the world had suddenly become too bright to look at. He was speechless with pleasure.

"Vern," she said, and then she added the most beautiful sentence Vern had ever heard, one he would never forget: "You are a hero."

Family Favourites

Vicki Blossom was fixing breakfast. She was fixing the family favourite: fried shredded wheat. She softened the shredded wheat in hot milk, and then she put it on the griddle, flattened it with the spatula, and fried it. The Blossoms ate it with lots of syrup.

"Anybody want seconds?" she asked. When nobody answered, she looked around. She couldn't believe it. "Nobody?"

The three kids shook their heads.

"Well, all right. I'll save these for Pap."

At the moment Pap was off looking for Mud. All day yesterday and at dawn today he'd been in his pick-up truck, riding around town, whistling out of the window for Mud.

"You're just wasting gas, Pap," Vicki had told him.

"Not if I find him," Pap answered. "It ain't wasted if I find him."

"Well, at least wait until the rain lets up."

"I can whistle for him in the rain good as I can in the sunshine."

And he had driven off, whistling. The rain coming in the window poured down his wrinkled face.

151

"All we need is for you to catch pneumonia!" she called after him.

Vicki watched her children at the table. "Are you kids still moping about that ugly dog?" She shook her spatula at them.

The Blossom kids looked down at their plates to keep from meeting her eyes.

"I'm ashamed of you kids. Count your blessings, Pap's out of gaol, Junior's out of the hospital, I'm home, and you're moping about Mud. If you can't live without a dog, go to the pound and get another one."

"Mom!" Maggie looked up in shock. "That's a terrible thing to suggest."

"We could get a puppy," Junior said. He liked the idea. "A puppy is not a dog."

"It is, too, Junior," Maggie said. "Anyway, it's not our dog, Mom; it's Pap's. Mud lets us play with him, but he's Pap's dog. That's why I feel bad. Pap really loves Mud."

"Pap is old enough to hide his feelings. If he wouldn't go around with that long, sad face, looking like he'd lost his best friend, whistling out of the truck window like a lunatic, you wouldn't feel bad. Shoot, I felt bad leaving the rodeo. The rodeo's in my blood—you know that. But I didn't mope around, making everybody else feel bad too. Pap needs to grow up."

She slapped a flattened shredded wheat on her plate. It was one of the ones she had been saving for Pap. She sat at the table and ate it angrily,

152

without syrup, cutting it up so hard with her fork that pieces shot off the plate.

Mud was rolling in a patch of wet Bermuda grass. He nosed his way through, rubbing his stinging eyes against the cool grass. He had spent the past eight hours rolling in whatever he could find—moss, leaves, dirt, mud, a small stream, a bank of ferns. None of it got rid of the smell.

His eyes still felt scratchy, but at least he could see now. After the spray hit his face, his eyes had watered so much and so long that a lot of the irritation had been washed away.

He twisted over and rubbed the other side of his face. Then he got up and shook himself. He saw a stand of pine trees, and he went over and rubbed his face against the rough bark. Turning, he did the other side.

It was nice under the pines. The branches shielded him from the rain. Like Pap, Mud had never cared much for rain.

He lay down and rolled in the pine needles, nosing them from side to side, still trying to get the scent off his face.

He rested a moment. Mud was exhausted. He had not had a real meal in four days. His ribs showed through his fur.

Still, there was something comforting about lying under these particular pine trees. He had lain here before. Maggie had pushed him under here one hot summer afternoon and said, "Now you're the wolf and I'm Hiawatha. You stay under there until I come by and I don't see you and I don't know you're there. Pretend like you're going to eat me."

He had waited on the soft bed of needles— waited, without understanding why, for the okay to come out. With the memory growing sharper, urging him on, Mud squirmed out from under the branches. He stood for a moment, smelling the air.

Then he began to bark wildly as he bounded through the woods. He leapt over bushes, logs, the creek. He charged down the ravine, up the other side. His shrill barks rang through the woods and echoed. The sound was continuous, like the ringing of bells on a joyous occasion.

Together

"See if you can guess what this song is," Junior said. He put his harmonica in his mouth. He kept it on a string around his neck because of Ralphie's unfortunate experience. At least if he swallowed his harmonica, he could pull it back up.

"I'm tired of guessing," Maggie said. "Let Vern guess this one."

"They all sound the same to me," Vern said.

"No, this one's different."

Junior began to play.

Vicki Blossom was at the sink, washing the breakfast dishes. She had just opened the window, and she was the first to hear Mud's wild barking.

"Well, you kids can stop moping," she said over her shoulder. "I hear Mud."

She opened the back door and went out on the stoop, drying her hands. Maggie and Vern ran out too. Junior was desperately trying to manœuvre his wheelchair around the kitchen furniture.

"Wait for me! I want to see too!"

Mud came out of the trees like a streak; he tore up the incline where the Blossoms threw the garbage; he leapt over the old tractor. He headed for the house.

Vicki threw back her head. "Oh, Lord, he's been skunked. Get back in the house. Quick." She held her nose. "Get back, Maggie. Close the screen door. Quick! Junior, get out of the way. She spun his wheelchair around. "Close the door, Vern. Close it!" She reached around and slammed the door herself just as Mud hit the porch.

Mud leapt up and down, throwing himself at the door. His happy face appeared framed in the high glass pane every time he jumped.

When she had watched his face come into view seven or eight times, Maggie said, "I don't care. I'm going out."

She turned the knob and slipped through the door. "Me, too," Vern said.

"Well, you're not coming back in this house, either one of you, if I catch one whiff of skunk on you or your clothing."

"We know."

Maggie and Vern threw their arms around Mud.

"Well, they can split us up," Pap said. He was in the creek, washing Mud with heavy-duty detergent. "But we Blossoms always manage to get back together. That's the good thing about being a Blossom."

"One of the good things," Maggie said.

This was Mud's seventh bath. For the first two

or three he had spent a lot of time trying to get out or shake the soap off, but now he was resigned to being washed.

He stood without moving. His ears were flat against his head. His tail was between his legs. His eyes rolled occasionally up to Pap.

"I hate it as bad as you do," Pap told him.

Maggie and Vern sat on the bank, watching. Maggie had on another old outfit of Vern's, and her braids were wet. "Tomorrow," her mom had told her, "I'll make you a French braid. I learned how to do it in a beauty parlour in Pecos. Hey, maybe I'll go to work in a beauty parlour. That always was my second love."

Vern's hair was wet, too, combed with a parting. "You kids have got to start fixing yourselves up," their mom told them. "Maggie, I'm getting you some dresses."

"And cowboy boots."

"We'll see."

"Okay, Mud, that's probably about as good as we're going to do." Pap rinsed him off with a bucketful of water. Mud closed his eyes as Pap poured another bucket over his head.

"Go roll in the grass," Pap told him. As soon as Mud heard the word *go* he went.

He leapt up the bank and shook himself. Drops of water hit Maggie and Vern, and they turned their faces out of the way. Mud rolled in the grass. He got up, shook himself, rolled again.

Pap stepped out of the creek with the aid of a

157

small tree. Pap used trees like walking sticks. He pulled himself up the bank.

He said, "Vern, I noticed a lot of beer and pop cans when I was riding into town. After lunch, what say we go pick them up?"

"Fine with me," Vern said.

"Well," Pap straightened. "Let's go up to the house and see if we smell good enough to be allowed inside."

And with Mud leading the way, the Blossoms headed for home.

Some Other Titles by Betsy Byars

THE PINBALLS

Carlie has been suspicious of people ever since the day she was born. When she arrives at her new foster home Mrs Mason tells her she can help the two boys staying there but Carlie doesn't believe her.

Eventually Charlie learns that she *can* help Harvey and Thomas J just by being herself but it takes a long time . . .

ISBN: 0 435 12382 3

THE CARTOONIST

When Alfie is in his attic he can forget all about Mom and Pap arguing. In his attic Alfie can create his own secret world in his cartoons which he knows will make people laugh one day.

When Alfie hears that his brother, Bubba, is coming home to live in the attic it is the last straw. Then Alfie hits on a plan to make the attic his own for ever . . .

ISBN: 0 435 123858 8

THE EIGHTEENTH EMERGENCY

Mouse and Ezzie are armed with plans for seventeen emergencies. If they meet sharks in their swimming area or if one of them is bitten by a tarantula they know exactly what they'll do. But Mouse has no idea how to cope with the eighteenth and unexpected emergency. Marv Hammerman, the toughest boy in the school, is out to get him . . .

ISBN: 0 435 12383 1

General Editors: Anne and Ian Serraillier

Chinua Achebe Things Fall Apart
Douglas Adams The Hitchhiker's Guide to the Galaxy
Vivien Alcock The Cuckoo Sister; The Monster Garden; The Trial of Anna Cotman
Michael Anthony Green Days by the River
Bernard Ashley High Pavement Blues; Running Scared
J G Ballard Empire of the Sun
Stan Barstow Joby
Nina Bawden The Witch's Daughter; A Handful of Thieves; Carrie's War; The Robbers; Devil by the Sea; Kept in the Dark; The Finding; Keeping Henry
Judy Blume It's Not the End of the World; Tiger Eyes
E R Braithwaite To Sir, With Love
John Branfield The Day I Shot My Dad
F Hodgson Burnett The Secret Garden
Ray Bradbury The Golden Apples of the Sun; The Illustrated Man
Betsy Byars The Midnight Fox
Victor Canning The Runaways; Flight of the Grey Goose
John Christopher The Guardians; Empty World
Gary Crew The Inner Circle
Jane Leslie Conly Racso and the Rats of NIMH
Roald Dahl Danny, The Champion of the World; The Wonderful Story of Henry Sugar; George's Marvellous Medicine; The BFG; The Witches; Boy; Going Solo; Charlie and the Chocolate Factory; Matilda
Andrew Davies Conrad's War
Anita Desai The Village by the Sea
Peter Dickinson The Gift; Annerton Pit; Healer
Berlie Doherty Granny was a Buffer Girl
Gerald Durrell My Family and Other Animals
J M Falkner Moonfleet
Anne Fine The Granny Project
F Scott Fitzgerald The Great Gatsby
Anne Frank The Diary of Anne Frank

Leon Garfield Six Apprentices
Graham Greene The Third Man and The Fallen Idol; Brighton Rock
Marilyn Halvorson Cowboys Don't Cry
Thomas Hardy The Withered Arm and Other Wessex Tales
Rosemary Harris Zed
Rex Harley Troublemaker
L P Hartley The Go-Between
Esther Hautzig The Endless Steppe
Ernest Hemingway The Old Man and the Sea; A Farewell to Arms
Nat Hentoff Does this School have Capital Punishment?
Nigel Hinton Getting Free; Buddy; Buddy's Song
Minfong Ho Rice Without Rain
Anne Holm I Am David
Janni Howker Badger on the Barge; Isaac Campion
Kristin Hunter Soul Brothers and Sister Lou
Barbara Ireson (Editor) In a Class of Their Own
Jennifer Johnston Shadows on Our Skin
Toeckey Jones Go Well, Stay Well
James Joyce A Portrait of the Artist as a Young Man
Geraldine Kaye Comfort Herself; A Breath of Fresh Air
Clive King Me and My Million
Dick King-Smith The Sheep-Pig
Daniel Keyes Flowers for Algernon
Elizabeth Laird Red Sky in the Morning
D H Lawrence The Fox and The Virgin and the Gypsy; Selected Tales
Harper Lee To Kill a Mockingbird
Laurie Lee As I Walked Out One Midsummer Morning
Julius Lester Basketball Game
Ursula Le Guin A Wizard of Earthsea
C Day Lewis The Otterbury Incident
David Line Run for Your Life; Screaming High
Joan Lingard Across the Barricades; Into Exile; The Clearance; The File on Fraulein Berg
Penelope Lively The Ghost of Thomas Kempe
Jack London The Call of the Wild; White Fang
Lois Lowry The Road Ahead; The Woods at the End of Autumn Street

How many have you read?

By the Same Author

THE ROSARY
THE MISTRESS OF SHENSTONE
THE FOLLOWING OF THE STAR
THROUGH THE POSTERN GATE
THE UPAS TREE
THE BROKEN HALO
THE WALL OF PARTITION
RETURNED EMPTY
SHORTER WORKS
THE WHITE LADIES OF WORCESTER
GUY MERVYN

Returned Empty

Returned Empty

Returned Empty

By

Florence L. Barclay

Author of "The Rosary," etc.

LONDON

Putnam & Company

42, Great Russell Street

First Published	June	1920
Reprinted	July	1920
Popular Edition	October	1923
Reprinted	July	1924
Reprinted	March	1925
Reprinted	September	1926
Reprinted	May	1927
Reprinted	January	1929
Reprinted	June	1930
Reprinted	January	1933
Reprinted	May	1936
Reprinted	March	1940
Reprinted	September	1944
Reprinted	October	1946
Reprinted	March	1948

BR/BR

Printed in Great Britain by
Wyman & Sons, Ltd., London, Fakenham and Reading

To
CATHERINE

Lord Tennyson's poem, " Crossing the Bar,"
is printed by kind permission of
Messrs. Macmillan & Co.

CONTENTS

Contents

SCENE I

Glass With Care

SCENE I

GLASS WITH CARE

A LIMITLESS expanse of opal sea, calm and unruffled, reflecting the crimson and gold of the sky, as the sun went down behind pine woods and moors.

A clear-cut line of cliffs, rising sheer from the stretch of golden sands.

Whirling white wings, as the gulls, shrieking in hungry chorus, swooped to the fringe of the outgoing tide.

A narrow path, skirting the edge of the cliffs, all among the pungent fragrance of gorse and heather and yellow bracken.

Along this path, on a warm September evening, swung a solitary figure; a man with sad eyes, feeling himself a blot upon the landscape, yet drinking in every tint of sunset glory, every wild wonder of snowy wings, every whiff of crushed fragrance. And, as he walked, the water down below seemed to call to him in a silent chorus of sparkling voices : " This is the way to the City of Gold. Leap from the cliff ! Take to the waters ! This, and this only, is your road for Home."

It was the Lonely Man's thirtieth birthday. Nobody had wished him many happy returns of the day. Nobody knew that it was his birthday. He would not have known it himself had it not been for the soiled and faded label which he carried in his pocket-book : GLASS WITH CARE printed on one side ; and, on the other, RETURNED EMPTY. Beneath the former was written, in red ink : *Luke xii.* 6 ; beneath the latter : *September* 12, 1883.

This label had been tied to the helpless bundle left, thirty years before, on a doorstep in a London suburb, one moonless October night. The man-child, wailing forlornly in the calico wrappings, was obviously a month-old baby.

The matron of the Foundlings' Institution, to which a stalwart policeman carried the bundle, after she had handed over the infant to her most capable nurse to be washed and clothed and fed, carefully proceeded to examine the wrappings and the label.

The wrappings held no clue. No laundry marks were on the strips of calico sheeting; no fair linen or fine lace pointed to a stealthy removal from a palatial mansion to the cold comfort of the suburban doorstep. No jewelled locket held a young mother's wistful face, or a tress of golden hair. The lonely baby had arrived in the coarsest of unbleached calico sheeting. "Ten-three a yard," said the matron, and took up the label.

" 'Returned Empty.' Well, *that* he undoubtedly was, bless his poor little tummy! '*September the* 12*th*.' Just over a month ago. That must be his birthday, poor mite! 'Glass with care.' Well, I never! They might at least have chosen a label marked

'Perishable.' And what's written here?
'*Luke xii.* 6.' They had better have left the
Bible out of their wrong-doings."

The matron was thorough in the search
for a possible clue. She fetched a Bible
and looked up the reference.

"Are not five sparrows sold for two
farthings, and not one of them is forgotten
before God?"

"Well, I never!" said the matron. "So
they label that bonny boy a little worthless
sparrow!" The matron waxed eloquent in
her indignation. "This bit of flotsam on
life's ocean, this helpless waif, flung in its
cheap wrappings on the mercy of strangers,
is valued by those who forsook it at less
than the Jewish half-farthing!"

The chaplain had preached, quite lately,
on the fifth sparrow thrown in to make the
bargain. So, when he came for the christening, and names must be given to the
nameless, remembering the sermon and the
label, the matron "named this child," Luke
Sparrow.

Sometimes, laughing, they called him "Little Glass with Care," he was so easily troubled, so sensitive to harsh sounds or roughness of touch. His baby lip quivered so readily; his dark eyes became deep pools of silent misery. And in another sense he was like a glass, during his babyhood. His beautiful little face mirrored things not seen. He would turn away from toys, and lie gazing at the sunbeams or at as much as could be seen of the sky through the high windows; and sometimes he would stretch out his arms to nothingness, and, arching his little body, lift it almost off his mattress, as if in response to some yearning call of love.

The first word he spoke was "Coming." He would shout: "Coming! Coming!" when nobody had called. He turned, impatient, from kind bosoms ready to cuddle him; he slipped unresponsive from laps in which he might have nestled softly, and hurled himself where only hard boards received him, or a cold wall bruised his baby head.

" ' Now we see as in a mirror enigmas,' " quoted the matron, whose minister habitually preached from the Revised Version. "What are you trying to remember, you queer little Bundle of Mystery? Who calls, when you say ' Coming'? What waiting breast which is not here, makes you bump your poor little head against the wall ? "

But, by the time he was three years old, he had outlived even the matron's tenderness. His little heart opened to none of them. His grave, sweet beauty grew repellent. His solemn eyes looked past their most persuasive danglings. Poor little " Returned Empty ! " His body throve under their care. His spirit seemed to yearn for something they could not give. He was a lonely baby.

Years went by. He outgrew the nursery, and passed into the school. Steadily he worked his way to the top of each class and stayed there. He took very little account of his school-fellows. The cruel could not hurt him ; the friendly failed to reach him.

"First Prize ; Luke Sparrow."

He made his graceful, solemn bow, and took the book ; but his dark eyes, undazzled by the grand, gold chain, looked past the portly Mayor, and failed to see the smile of approval on the head-master's face ; his ears were deaf to the plaudits of assembled patrons and friends. He returned to his place, hugging this book. Nobody asked to see it ; he shewed it to nobody. He was a lonely little boy.

He preferred study involving solitude, to games which hurled him among companions of his own age. The chaplain took an interest in the queerly brilliant little mind, and gave the boy constant private coaching, with the result that he won a Grammar School scholarship, carrying advantages which he could not have enjoyed at the Foundlings' Institution.

Two passions at this time began to possess him, giving him his only thrills of pleasure. The first was his love of the water. He swam like a fish. The first time he went with the other boys to the swimming baths he stood on the edge watching the swimmers ; gazing, with brooding eyes at the water, as if striving to capture an evasive memory.

" Jump in, Sparrow ! " shouted the young master in charge. " There must always be a beginning. Don't funk it ! "

The lithe body quivered all over, a ripple of muscles under the smooth skin. He walked down the steps with the sudden alertness of one awaking from a long dream, slipped into the water, and, as it lapped around him, glided forward and swam from one end of the bath to the other, with the ease and grace of a little water animal.

They called him the Frog. They called him the Minnow. Later on, they called him the Sea-Lion. It mattered nothing to him

what they called him. He swam for the
sheer joy of it. He felt more alive in the
water than on land. He seemed to come
nearer to finding something he had been
seeking all his short life.

His first swim in the sea brought the
swift resolve to eschew heaven. "Why?"
asked another boy, to whom in an unusual
moment of expansiveness he confided
as they shared a towel, this momentous
decision, "Because," said Luke, "once
we get there, the Bible says there shall be
no more sea."

His other passion was for gazing in at
windows, from the outside, after dark,
when firelight gleamed fitfully on shining
furniture; when unknown people sat talking, and smiling, and handing each other
cups of tea; when they lighted lamps and
candles, forgetting to draw the curtains
and leaving the windows unshuttered.

When he left school and was launched
on life, a lonely youth, to fend for

himself, earning enough by his pen for his own modest needs, rousing himself to a few hours of brilliant work if he wanted new books, new clothes, or a complete holiday— this strange fascination grew. A hunger possessed him to look in at other people's windows. He would walk miles to satisfy this craving. Out into the country, where farm kitchens sent a ruddy glow across the fields ; where cottage windows gleamed like friendly stars. He would draw near, avoiding kennels and gravel paths, and feast his eyes on cosy rooms ; husbands and wives, seated in easy chairs at the end of the day's work ; fathers and mothers, among their children ; comfortable cats, purring before the fire ; faithful dogs, suddenly alert, ears pricking, eyes on the window pane.

He had no wish to be within. His pleasure was to look in from outside, as a being from another world, with no personal share in this life's loves and joys, with an insatiable desire to witness them.

Sometimes the inmates of these lighted rooms chanced to look up and see the strained face and sombre eyes gazing through the window. Then they would make a movement of fear or of anger; or a kindly move, as if to ask him in. In either case he would turn away quickly and disappear in the darkness. He had no wish to enter, he had no desire to share their joys. He only asked to view them from without.

Yet gradually the conviction grew within him that this passion was a quest: that some day he would look through a window and see a room which should seem to him that thing he had never known—Home.

Grand interiors he saw, in London streets and squares; glimpses of tasteful furniture, art treasures, a suitable setting for perfectly gowned grace and beauty; swiftly concealed by the drawing of velvet curtains.

It angered him that the illusive sense of home drew nearer to him in these fitful visions of wealth and loveliness than when he looked into humbler and more simple houses. All his sympathies were with those who worked and toiled, living by the soil and upon it.

He liked the farmer who drank ale from a brown jug, while his pleasant wife enjoyed her dish of tea.

Peering through area railings into the basement of London houses, he liked the stout cook who stood before a glowing kitchen range, toasting-fork in hand, flinging remarks over her portly print shoulder to the pretty young housemaid, perched on the kitchen table, swinging her feet and darning a stocking.

He loved the grey parrot with a naughty eye, no doubt banished from the drawing-room on account of its language, sidling up and down its perch, in the cage under the window. He felt sure it was making valuable additions to its vocabulary, what time the heat of the fire on one side and the flippant attitude of the pretty housemaid on the other, annoyed the stout cook.

He disliked the beautiful woman in the room above, who reclined among silken cushions, giving languid orders to a deferential butler, then waved an impatient command to the footman to draw the curtains. Yet the drawing of those curtains shut out the haunting sense of home, which had grown within him as he watched the woman among the silken cushions.

He returned to his solitary rooms and spent the evening writing an article in which he decried the idle rich and extolled the humble poor. Yet, while he wrote, he wondered, half wistfully, who he might be who had the right to come in and fill the armchair drawn close to that couch of silken cushions. He wondered this; and wondering, ceased writing, lit his pipe and took to dreaming.

He was a lonely youth.

By degrees his gift of descriptive writing won him an acknowledged place in the world of journalism. He was trusted by an important newspaper to observe and record various historic scenes in the great metropolis—a royal funeral ; a coronation ; the city's welcome to a famous general.

He wrote with a peculiar detachment, never obtruding his own personality ; viewing events in their larger meaning, as well as in careful completeness of minor detail ; yet with no throb of human sentiment, no personal touch of intimate feeling.

Later on, he went in a similar capacity to India, and wrote one of the finest descriptions on record of the royal Durbar.

He moved amid scenes of varied interest ; he made many acquaintances, but no close friends.

His distant travels accomplished, he would return to his comfortless rooms, and work in solitude.

That within him which might have responded to love, and leapt into intimacy, seemed shut away behind prison bars. When Love drew near, he could but look forth with haunted eyes, watching while Love, rebuffed, moved sadly away.

He was a lonely man.

When he allowed himself a holiday, he packed a small knapsack, went by the fastest route possible to Scotland, Cornwall, Devon or Norfolk—anywhere where he could find a rugged coast; long stretches of gorse and heather; villages, which he could reach by nightfall.

Each morning he would be on the shore at sunrise, swimming, with strong, eager strokes, up the golden path toward the dazzling glory of the rising sun. Or, if he chanced, at close of day, to find himself where the coast faced westward, he would slip in to the water at sunset and glide, with slow, dreamy motion and folded arms, up the crimson way toward the setting sun.

No day seemed complete to him unless it began and ended in the sea.

So, on this 12th of September, though the sun was sinking behind distant moors,

when the waters called, he made his way
down the cliff, walked half a mile or so
along the shore until he found cover among
rocks; then swam swiftly out to sea, re-
capturing the crimson ball as it disappeared
behind the pine woods.

When he turned for a last sight of it, he
noticed a fine old house, standing castle-like
on the summit of the cliff, just above the
rocks beside which he had left his clothes.
It had not been in view when he had quitted
the high path for the beach and the lee
of the cliffs.

He swam back to the shore, dressed,
lighted his pipe, and sat among the rocks
till twilight fell.

The moon appeared, a huge yellow ball,
rising out of the sea.

He found himself humming an old song
he had picked up the year before, while
on a walking tour through Brittany.

> " Au clair de la lune,
>   Mon ami Pierrot !
> Prête-moi ta plume.
>   Pour écrire un mot.

Ma chandelle est morte,
Je n'ai plus de feu !
Ouvre-moi ta porte
Pour l'amour de Dieu ! "

The pathetic words, and the melancholy air, seemed strangely suited to his mood and to the place.

The twilight deepened.

He rose and climbed a zigzag path leading to the top of the cliff.

" Ma chandelle est morte,
Je n'ai plus de feu ! "

He reached the top, and passed through an iron gate.

" Ouvre-moi ta porte,
Pour l'amour de Dieu ! "

Almost before he realised that he was trespassing, he was standing on the lawn of the house he had seen from the sea.

Ma chandelle est morte,
Je n'ai plus de feu;
Ouvre-moi ta porte,
Pour l'amour de Dieu."

...the pathetic words, and the melancholy
...it, seemed strangely suited to his mood
and to the place.

The twilight deepened.

He rose and climbed a zigzag path leading to the top of the cliff.

"Ma chandelle est morte,
Je n'ai plus de feu,"

He reached the top, and passed through
an iron gate.

"Ouvre-moi ta porte,
Pour l'amour de Dieu!"

Almost before he realised that he was
trespassing, he was standing on the lawn
of the house he had seen from the sea.

SCENE II
The Unexpected Welcome

SCENE II

The Unexpected Welcome

Scene II

THE UNEXPECTED WELCOME

A VERANDA, overhung by rambler roses, ran the full length of the front of the house.

Through the diamond panes of low lattice windows, the fitful glow of firelight gleamed.

The Lonely Man hesitated, half turned away, then, drawn by an irresistible attraction, stepped on to the veranda, stood in the shadow, and looked in at a window.

The room was so large, and its occupants so far from the windows, that the silent intruder had small need to fear detection.

His first furtive glance into the interior awakened, with a sudden throb, more strongly than ever before, that illusive sense of home.

He drew nearer.

A long, low room; the many windows running half the length of the veranda, a cushioned window seat beneath them. A door, on his left, opened on to the veranda. At the opposite side of the room, another door, standing ajar, led into a large hall. At the top of the room, on his right, a log fire burned in the huge fireplace. The leaping flames illumined the oak panelling and played on the carved beams in the ceiling. Persian rugs, in soft tints of blue and rose, lay upon the polished parquet.

A couch, on the further side of the fireplace, and at right-angles to it, faced the windows. In the centre, opposite the hearth, stood two large easy chairs.

These chairs were occupied by a young man in tweeds and shooting-boots—who lay back luxuriously with legs outstretched, as if long tramping in the heather had earned him a welcome rest—and by a very lovely girl, whose smiles and looks of happy tenderness were divided between the sturdy figure in the other chair, and a very small boy in Highland dress, who darted to and fro between them, trying to intercept a ball as they threw it to one another; a brave little figure, in tartan kilt and velvet jacket; his brown curls tumbled, his dark eyes shining, as he fell, over his father's legs, headlong into his mother's lap.

One casement stood open, and the lonely watcher could hear their merry laughter and the boy's triumphant shout as he snatched the ball from his mother's hand.

Holding it above his head, he danced out into the middle of the room, in full view of the windows.

The watching eyes narrowed in puzzled wonder.

Why was that leaping figure so familiar? The two in the chairs awakened no memories. The lovely woman, with her fair skin and coils of shining hair; the man, long-limbed, freckled and ruddy—total strangers both. Yet this child, who called them "Father" and "Mother," this little dark head, brown, oval face, black level brows? Where had he met the imp before?

His mind went back some twenty odd years to the Christmas after his eighth birthday. The kind Mayor had made a feast at the Townhall for the children from the Institution. They were given funny dresses to wear. A Highland dress was found for him, kilt and plaid and dirk complete. The little black velvet jacket had silver buttons with thistles on them. Some ladies talked about him. They said: "With those wonderful dark eyes and curls, he should have come as the Black Prince. Who is he?" They kissed him and gave him chocolates. He hated being kissed; but he liked the chocolates; and he liked being called the Black Prince. At one end of the hall there was a long mirror. He slipped away and stood before it. He had never before seen himself full length in a mirror. He held the box of chocolates above his head——

Why—yes! This little boy with the ball

was an exact replica of the figure he had seen reflected in the mirror ; a replica of himself.

He felt dizzy—shaken.

He was turning away ; but at that moment, the hall beyond was illuminated.

Something moved across it.

A woman appeared in the open doorway —an arresting figure—a woman with snow-white hair, tall, stately, matronly ; extraordinarily beautiful, with a calm, melancholy beauty ; a woman well past middle age, yet with soft white skin, unwrinkled ; upright carriage ; a noble, gracious personality.

" In the dark, children ? " she said ; then put out her hand, and the room flashed into light.

" Grannie ! " shouted the boy, and ran to meet her.

With her hand upon his shoulder, she moved slowly into the middle of the room.

The young man half rose, offering his chair.

" Do not move, Colin," she said and went to the couch.

The boy climbed up beside her, nestling his dark curls into the lace at her bosom. She put her arm about him with a gesture infinitely tender and protective.

The younger woman spoke. "Colin and I were lazing in the firelight, mother. Then Nigel arrived with his ball, and forced us to be energetic."

The watcher at the window pressed closer to the pane. In the fascination of the scene he forgot to fear discovery.

By the brighter light the couple appeared older than he had at first thought them. She was probably his own age, even older; her husband, two or three years her senior. She had inherited her mother's remarkable beauty. It was good to see them together. The one revealed the youthful loveliness of the past; the other promised the maturer beauty yet to come; and both were very good to look upon.

The man reclining in the chair between them, gazed intently at his own boots. He turned them from side to side, as the flame played upon them, and examined them critically. Then he thrust his hands deep into his breeches' pockets, stretched his long legs to the fire, and stared at his boots with whole-hearted admiration.

For the first time in all the long years, the Lonely Man without, yearned to be within. His loneliness seized and shook him. All his searching, all his watching, all his hungry, forlorn hours, seemed to have reached their culmination. This—this, at last, was Home! Yet he stood outside, as a watcher from another world; he had no part nor lot in the love and comfort within.

His yearning gaze was fixed upon the central figure in the scene. Yes, she would always be the central figure in any scene. In court or cottage alike, she would be queen.

No wonder his little double dashed forward when she said: "In the dark, children?" If *that* voice could have called him, when he was a lonely little boy, how gladly he—who never came when he was

called—would have shouted "Coming!"
and flown to her embrace.

He looked at the dark head, so like his
own, nestling against the softness of her
breast. He could see her bosom rise and
fall, in steady, rhythmic breathing, beneath
the little olive cheek. Dark lashes veiled
the bright brown eyes. Nigel was growing
sleepy. What wonder, in such " sweet
security."

Nigel's parents talked together.

She—sat silent, looking down at the small
face against her breast.

It struck him that there was an aloofness
about her, a loneliness which almost
matched his own. Tragedy had laid its
mark upon that noble face ; a sorrow borne
in patient silence ; an agony unshared ; a
grief too deep to be plumbed by human
sympathy.

It seemed to the Lonely Man that his loneliness would be easier to bear, for having
looked upon her ; his " Returned Empty "
life would hold more possibility of fulness ;

his " Glass with care" would be less
sensitively brittle, for having seen the
mastered tragedy in that calm face, crowned
by the silvered hair.

One final look; then he must turn away
and be lost again in the outer darkness.

His face was close against the glass. His
hungry eyes peered through.

At that moment she raised her head,
looked straight across to the window, and
saw him.

He could not move.

He could not look away. Her eyes gazed
into his; right into his, and held them.

She sat perfectly still.

The hand stroking little Nigel's leg,
paused.

The boy's lashes lay upon his cheek.
He stirred uneasily. The hand stroked
again.

Her face blanched to ashen whiteness;
then the delicate colour flooded it once more.

Still her eyes held him.

At last her lips moved, silently. They formed one word : " Wait."

Presently she rose.

Nigel rubbed his eyes, leapt from the sofa, and found his ball.

She moved toward the window.

The man without stepped back into the shadow.

Nigel had flung the ball at his mother, and fallen over his father's legs. The three were laughing and shouting together.

She came to the open casement, pushed it wider and leaned out.

She spoke very quietly, into the fragrant darkness; the faintest whisper, yet he heard.

" I was expecting you " . . . Her voice was like the night-wind in the tops of the pine trees; soft as a sigh, and full of mystery. " Do not go . . . You will find a chair in the corner on your right. Wait there until I am alone."

She drew back into the room, and closed the casement.

He sank into the chair and sat there in the silence, listening to the beating of his heart. It sounded like heavy breakers pounding on the rocks below.

He sank into the chair and sat there in the silence, listening to the beating of his heart. It sounded like heavy breakers pounding on the rocks below.

SCENE III

The Expected Guest

SCENE III

THE EXPECTED GUEST

HE sat very still, and waited.

He had miles to walk before he could reach an inn ; but food and a night's lodging seemed unnecessary considerations in this strange hour.

She had asked him to wait until she should be alone ; and he waited.

A motor came to the other side of the house ; panted impatiently for five minutes ; then sped away into the distance.

He stood up and looked into the room.

It was empty. Fresh logs had been thrown upon the fire. The door into the hall was shut.

Even as he looked, it opened.

An elderly butler appeared, walked forward into the room, hesitated ; then

advanced to the garden door, touched a
switch, and a couple of hanging lanterns
shed a soft light over the veranda.   He
stood in the doorway, as if momentarily
uncertain ;   then saw the chair and its
occupant in the corner on his left, came
over to it and delivered his message, in
deferential tones, without lifting his eyes.

"Her ladyship bids me say, sir, that
dinner will be served in half an hour.   If you
will follow me, I will show you to your
room."

"To my room ? "

"Yes, sir.   Her ladyship understood you
would be able to dine and sleep."

The butler moved to the door, held it
wide and waited.   There was nothing for
it, but to rise and enter.

So the man who had all his life looked
in from without now stepped over the
threshold and found himself within.

Feeling keenly alive and yet as if moving
in a vivid dream, Luke Sparrow walked

across the room, and followed the butler into the brightly lighted hall, and up a wide staircase.

On a table in the hall stood a box of library books, addressed with a brush, in very black ink. Before he realised what he was doing he had read the name—

LADY TINTAGEL

He repeated it to himself as he mounted the stairs. It awakened memories of Camelot. He had never heard of it as a family name; but it seemed in keeping with this romance of an unexpected visit, as an expected guest.

At the top of the stairs the butler paused to say: "Her ladyship desires that you will please yourself, sir, as to whether you dress or not."

Luke smiled. His knapsack held a clean shirt, a razor, a comb, a toothbrush, and half a dozen handkerchiefs.

"I am doing a walking tour," he said.

" You might explain to her ladyship that I have nothing with me but bare necessaries in a small knapsack."

The butler opened a door, switched on the light and stood aside that he might enter.

" You will find all you need here, sir. The door to the left leads into a bath-room. A gong will sound at eight. It is now half-past seven. If you should require anything more, will you be so good as to ring, sir ? " He retired, closing the door softly behind him.

Luke looked around and laughed. He wondered what on earth he could find to ring for, which was not already there !

He walked over to the dressing-table on which were silver-backed brushes, ivory razors, silver-topped bottles !

Laid out upon the bed was a complete suit of dress clothes.

If this was " Colin's " room, he certainly did himself well ! If these were " Colin's " clothes they certainly would not fit him !

Laughing again—he who never laughed

—he turned to the bed, flung off his rough Norfolk jacket, and slipped on the smooth black coat with its silk lining. It fitted him perfectly; and he was fastidious about the cut of his clothes.

Should he ? . . . Not he! He would never wear another man's garments. He would never stand in another man's shoes. If Lady Tintagel asked him to dine, she must have him as he was. If the lovely daughter looked askance at him, she must learn to understand that you don't carry a dress suit in a knapsack.

But the bath ? Yes, rather! That was quite another matter. His long sea swims had made him feel like a kipper.

What a bath-room! Every muscle relaxed in the steaming hot water. A bottle of fragrant aromatic stuff stood temptingly handy. He poured it in, and luxuriated. "Colin" must feel a god, with all this at his command, whenever he came in fagged. He must descend on his admiring womenfolk like a giant refreshed.

A cold shower—and then he blessed heaven he had put a clean shirt in his knapsack.

"Colin's" ivory-handled razors made shaving a positive pastime.

One moment of indecision, as he caught sight of the dress suit upon the bed. Strange that it should fit. He remembered the beautiful rooms downstairs. He would be decidedly out of the picture in his tweeds. He remembered the full-length mirror at the Mayor's party. "He should have come as the Black Prince." How he had enjoyed the remark! His first lesson in vanity. He smiled to think how often he had repeated it to himself, and postured in his shabby little suits. Do people realise how inordinately vain a small boy can be ? . . . Should he ! No ! That was a fancy-dress masquerade ; and so would this be. Whatever anybody said, whatever anybody thought, he must meet Lady Tintagel clad at least in the raiment of his own self-respect and independence. It was not as though he had arrived soaked through and had had to borrow dry things. He brushed his old tweeds vigorously with " Colin's " silver-backed clothes-brush.

A gong boomed sonorously through the house.

As he walked down the stairs he was still thinking, with dreamlike persistence, of the dress difficulty. " I shall say : ' Excuse this rig. One travels light on a walking tour.' "

In the hall the butler waited.

" This way, sir."

though he had arrived soaked through and had had to borrow dry things. He brushed his old tweeds vigorously with " Colin's " silver-backed clothes-brush.

A gong boomed sonorously through the house.

As he walked down the stairs he was still thinking with dreamlike persistence of the "chess difficulty." " I shall say, ' Excuse this rig.' One travels light on a walking tour."

In the hall the butler waited.

" This way, sir."

SCENE IV

The Prison Bars Dissolve

THE PRISON BARS DISSOLVE

LADY TINTAGEL was alone.

She stood at the far end of the drawing-room.

When he entered she was leaning against the mantelpiece, looking down into the fire.

She turned, still gripping the marble edge with her left hand.

She wore a gown of trailing black velvet and stood on a white Angora rug.

Miles of rose carpet lay between him and the fireplace.

He seemed to be walking uphill, as he came towards her.

When he reached the rug at last, he and she seemed to be standing together on the summit of a delectable mountain. His mind still ran on his unsuitable attire, but he forgot the sentence he had prepared.

" I couldn't," was his lame apology.

She looked at him and smiled. " *You*—wouldn't," she said.

There was such complete understanding in the grave regard of her kind eyes, in the low tones of her voice, so sweet and full of music.

It was all strangely intimate. As he stood beside her, lines he had heard years before flashed into his mind.

> " Two men looked out through prison bars ;
> One saw mud ; the other, stars."

Hitherto he had seen mud—always mud. In her presence he realised the possibility of seeing stars—undreamed-of stars.

And his prison bars themselves seemed vanishing.

Something captive in him broke its chains and leapt out into liberty.

And still she spoke no word ; but her eyes dwelt on him with that all-enveloping, comprehending look of tenderness.

An unspoken sentence seemed to hang

suspended. The silence was tense with it, as when a great orchestra, ready to sound the opening strain of a mighty symphony, waits, with eye, hand, and ear alert, for the first beat of the lifted baton.

But on the instant, came an anti-climax.

"Dinner is served, my lady," announced a deferential voice.

She laughed. "I suppose one *must* eat," she said; and his common sense wondered why she said it, and why the same thought, unspoken, had been in his own mind.

She laid her hand within his arm, and they moved slowly down the room together. Walking so with her, he noted that she was slightly taller than he. She leaned on him. He felt vividly alive. Where was his shell—his shell of morbid reserve, in which he had hidden himself since his babyhood?

He tried to ask her how it came about that she had been expecting him; but something restrained the question.

He wanted to tell her all about himself,

right from the beginning; all he had thought, and felt, and suffered; his shrinking from intimacy with his fellow-men; his loneliness; his shameful habit—he knew, now, that it was shameful—of looking in, unseen, at other people's windows, his half-unconscious belief that some day he would look in, out of the darkness, and see a room which his spirit would acclaim as home; and how, to-day—at last—But he could not tell her that! Yes, he could! He could tell her anything. She would understand. And when his confession was over, he would kneel before her—as a tired little boy might kneel at his mother's knees at bedtime—and say his prayers. Then she would lay her hands upon his head, and Divine forgiveness and benediction would be his.

They were crossing the hall. The butler stood at the dining-room door.

"After dinner," she said, "you must tell me all."

SCENE V

"I have Waited So Long!"

Scene V

"I HAVE WAITED SO LONG!"

THE round table was laid for two.

"I thought——" he said.

"Colin and Eva ? No ; their home is twelve miles from here. They were spending the afternoon with me. I live alone."

"I thought I was using your son-in-law's room."

"No," she said, "oh, no ! That room——" she paused. "The room you used—is my husband's dressing-room. Since I lost him, it has been kept exactly as he left it. For over thirty years it has looked, each day, just as if he had used it the day before. It did not give you the feeling of a disused apartment ? "

"No," he said ; "I thought——"

"You thought it was Colin's ? No ; Colin

has never been into that room. In fact, none enter there. It is a sanctuary of mine."

Her beautiful eyes were on his face as she said the words, full of an expression which he failed to fathom. He wondered why he should have been ushered into a sanctuary forbidden to others. Yet was he not, also, prepared to admit her into the sanctuary of his inner life, to which none had ever gained admission ?

The presence of the old man-servant, who did not leave the room, restrained more intimate conversation. He found himself wondering what they would say when at last they were really alone.

She talked of the beauty of the surrounding country; the wild hills, the heather; the pine woods, full of health-giving fragrance.

He told her of his walking tours.

"It is the only holiday I care for; to walk and walk, alone with Nature, from sunrise to sunset. Usually I reach an inn,

by nightfall; but it does not trouble me
if I don't. On warm nights, I would just
as soon sleep in the open." He looked up,
with the rare smile which softened his face
into extraordinary sweetness. "I am
afraid you are harbouring a tramp, Lady
Tintagel."

She met the smile with her own. "Am
I?" Her voice dropped very low. "My
tramp has tramped a long way to reach
harbour."

"A long way? I seem to have been walking all my life, just that I might reach here
to-night."

With a swift movement, she leaned forward and laid her hand on his.

"Wait!" she said.

It was the first time she had touched his
hand with hers.

An unexpected emotion awoke within
him. It was as if she had pressed an
electric switch, as he had seen her do when
entering the darkening room. His inner
being seemed flooded with light. His cold,

patient apathy quickened suddenly into impatience. He forgot conventions. He lost control of himself. He threw common sense to the winds. He caught the hand she had withdrawn, and gripped it.

"I can't wait," he said. "I have waited so long. I want to talk to you."

He felt like a headstrong boy who refuses to be good. He felt like a lover who suddenly gives way to the desire, cost what it may, to master his mistress. He felt like a drowning man catching at a rope. He felt like nothing he had ever felt before. And it soothed him to see this stately woman quiver and turn pale. Serve her right! What was she doing to him? Why did her touch go to his brain like the instant intoxication of champagne to a starving man? He felt reckless. Devil take the consequences! He couldn't play-act any more.

She rose at once. His obvious emotion restored her self-control.

"Come," she said quietly. Then to the

old man-servant, discreetly busying himself at the sideboard: "Serve the fruit and coffee in the Oak Room, Thomas."

Even while he blindly followed her, Luke felt a moment of surprise that the order received no deferential acknowledgment. He glanced at the man. Tears were running down his furrowed cheeks.

Strange—even where all was strange. Why should their emotion move this carefully trained automaton?

Lady Tintagel took up a wrap as they passed through the hall, went straight through the Oak Room, and out at the door leading on to the veranda.

SCENE VI

" Sunset and Evening Star "

SCENE VI

"SUNSET AND EVENING STAR"

THE moon had mounted into the heavens, and now cast a path of silver light across the sea.

They stood together looking down upon it.

"I came that way," he said. "The waters called me from the cliff top at sunset. I walked along the shore for half a mile or so, then found some handy rocks, stripped in their shelter, and swam out, far and fast, until the sun rose again, for me, behind the pine woods. As I swam back to shore I saw this house, for the first time. Later I found the zigzag path, climbed it, and stood upon the lawn. Twilight had fallen suddenly; a chill was in the air. I saw the fitful glow of firelight through the windows. The darkness came so quickly, I did not fear detection. I crossed the

73

lawn and stood on the veranda. I watched
the three at play by the log fire. The room
grew darker. I turned to go. Then you
came in, and flashed all into light. I stayed
—you bid me stay. And here I am. But I
came to you, in the sunset, from the sea."

" I thought as much," she said. " 'Sunset
and evening star, and one clear call for me.'
Do you know Tennyson's great crowning
poem ? Will you repeat it as we stand
here ? It was so strongly in my mind as I
watched the sunset. I think that was why
I was so sure you would come to-night."

" Yes, I know the lines," he answered.
" They have always held for me an extraordinary appeal. But how came you to be
expecting me—to-night, or any night ? "

" Repeat them. We have all the night for
questions ; but this moment will not come
again."

She slipped her hand within his arm. He
laid his own upon it and did as she asked.
And, as he repeated Tennyson's noble lines,
the tumult within his spirit ceased.

The stillness, all about them, was complete ; broken only by the music of his voice.

Sunset and evening star,
  And one clear call for me.
And may there be no moaning of the bar,
  When I put out to sea.

But such a tide as moving seems asleep,
  Too full for sound and foam,
When that which drew from out the boundless deep
  Turns again home.

Twilight and evening bell,
  And after that the dark ;
And may there be no sadness of farewell,
  When I embark ;

For tho' from out our bourne of Time and Place
  The flood may bear me far,
I hope to see my Pilot face to face,
  When I have crossed the bar.

A long silence. Then : " I have no pilot," he said. " I drift rudderless. I am bound to make shipwreck on the bar."

She did not seem to hear his words. Her mind was far away. Her eyes were on the sea, gazing upon that path of shimmering light.

" Nigel," she said, " there *was* no farewell

—no farewell, belovèd ; but oh, the dark—
the dark—the dark ! "

He wondered to whom she spoke. He
tightened his hold upon her hand and stood
silent.

" ' The Lord gave and the Lord hath
taken away.' Each evening I stood here
and said those words. If I could have
added : ' Blessed be the Name of the Lord,'
the darkness might have lightened. But I
could not ; and it still was dark."

He asked himself what awful memory of
sorrow brought that horror of anguish to
her face. But the moment kept him silent.
He could not speak.

" Oh, cruel sea ! " she moaned. " You
took my All—my All."

She shivered, and he folded her wrap
more closely around her.

Then she turned to him, and the look of
anguish passed. There was gladness in her
eyes.

" Come in," she said. " Let us come in ;
and shut the door."

SCENE VII

"And After That—the Dark"

SCENE VII

"AND AFTER THAT—THE DARK"

"NOW," said Lady Tintagel, as he put down his empty coffee-cup, "you may talk. There is no further need to wait."

"I want to tell you things from the beginning," he said. "Will it bore you if I begin at the beginning?"

"You could not bore me; and I would not miss one moment of the beginning. Tell me all."

"My name is Luke Sparrow, so named by the matron of the Foundlings' Institution to which I was carried when a month old, or thereabouts, by the arm of the Law. I began life on a doorstep—a suburban doorstep. I have never known home, or kith, or kin. Like Melchisedec of old, I am without father, without mother, without

79

descent ; but there the resemblance ends ; for Melchisedec was King of Salem, which is King of Peace, whereas I, from my infancy, have been possessed by a most restless demon. I was ' Returned Empty ' and marked ' Glass with Care '——"

"Returned Empty ? " There was horror in her voice. "What—what *do* you mean ? "

"The label," he said ; "the label pinned to the unwanted bundle had, printed in bold letters, on one side : RETURNED EMPTY, under which somebody who knew it, had written presumably, the date of my birth. On the other side was printed GLASS WITH CARE, beneath which the same careful person had taken the trouble to write a Bible reference, most explicitly explaining the exact value of the said bundle : *Luke xii.* 6. 'Are not five sparrows sold for two farthings ? ' This apt quotation inspired the matron on christening Sunday, to bestow upon me the name of Luke Sparrow. She was a good woman and meant well. But it was, ever after, a standing joke at the institution."

"Not one of them is forgotten before God," said Lady Tintagel.

"Yes, I know. But the close of the verse did not appear to be applicable, the bundle not containing a genuine sparrow, but merely a lonely little human child, 'Returned Empty.'"

"Returned?" she said; "Empty!" There was tragedy in her voice.

He laughed. "Yes; *very* empty—so the nurses said. Well, it was a bad beginning. The physical emptiness was soon remedied; but the mental and spiritual void remained unfilled. I've lived an utterly lonely life; and the misery of it was, I didn't seem able to accept companionship; I had no capacity for friendship, no wish for home-life. I have always been seeking, seeking, seeking for something I could not find. Lots of people wanted to be friendly; heaps of people tried to be kind; but I could not take their friendship, or accept their kind-

ness.   To misquote a well-known saying,
I was ' *in* the world but not *of* the world.'
And then I had a vice."

" A vice ? "   Her eyes, which never left
his face, darkened with apprehension.

" Yes ; a vice.   Oh, not drink, or drugs,
or other depravity.   I have kept my body
sane and clean, and without much effort
either.   I love the sea too well, and swim
in it too often, for any form of moral squalor
to have a chance."

" Squalor ! " she exclaimed, with a fine
disdain.   " *You* would have had no need for
squalor, you beautiful boy !   All women
must have loved you."

" Boy ? "   He laughed.   " Good Lord !
I was never a boy !   I was born with a
grown-up soul.   Yes, they were kind ; but I
wanted none of their kindness.   All women
were to me mere shadows.   Love never
called to me."

" The vice ? " she said.   " What was it ? "

" A mental thing.   A morbid craving to
look on at other people's joys ; to view

them without sharing them; an absolute hunger to see home life, though I had none of my own. This led me to the low-down practice of prowling about after dark, peering in at lighted windows, like a lonely soul from another world, spying on bliss he might not share. I began it as quite a little chap, peeping and running away. The passion grew as I grew. When my day's work was over, I would walk miles to stalk unshuttered windows. Many a time I have narrowly escaped being run in as a probable burglar. Many a fright I have given to innocent people who looked up suddenly and surprised my uncanny face pressed against the glass. I know now what I was seeking. In some sub-conscious part of me I knew that somewhere in the world was a window through which I should look and see at last a room which should be HOME.

"So I prowled on. I was prowling to-night. But I never before wanted to be invited to enter. I preferred to be outside. And—until to-night—I never realised what a low-down habit it was. To my morbid emptiness it seemed no wrong toward happy people, that I should just look upon their joys."

"But why to-night?"

"Ah, because all is different. You have done something to me; I don't know what, or why. Something in your sub-consciousness must have reached mine. You have burst the bars of my prison and set my spirit free. I shall leave here and go back to the world, a man among men. Hitherto I have felt—do you know the weird Schubert song?—a Doppelgänger. Good Lord, the horror of it! But you have broken the spell. I don't know how you did it. Perhaps it was because you asked me in."

"Why did you come in?" she whispered; "You, who always preferred to remain outside."

"Dare I tell you?" he asked. "Will you think it awful cheek? It was because—at last—at last—it was Home."

The woman on the couch opened wide her arms and leaned towards him with a movement of extraordinary tenderness. Her face was illumined by a radiance almost unearthly in its sublime joy.

" It *was* Home," she said. " It *is* Home. Ah, do you not remember, belovèd ? Never call yourself Luke Sparrow again. Never call yourself a foundling—you, whom I have found at last ! I can tell you your name, if there be still need to tell it : Nigel Guido Cardross Tintagel."

" What ? " The blood leapt into his face. His outstretched hands almost met hers. " Are you—are *you*—my mother ? "

" No, belovèd, no ! Oh, Nigel, think again ! Remember ! You *must* remember ! "

His hands clutched his knees. He looked full into her eyes ; a long, steady gaze.

At last : " I remember nothing," he said. " You will have to tell me. I would to God you were my mother. But, if that may not be, then—in Heaven's name what are you to me ? "

Her voice was a pæan of triumphant joy.
" I am your wife."

The man in the chair sat before her,
petrified. His hands gripped his knees.
Twice he essayed to speak; but no sound
would pass his lips.

At length : " Great God ! " he said :
" Am I mad, or are you ? "

" Nigel," she said, " my dearest, you have
come back to me. My boundless love, my
desperate grief, my passionate prayers,
have brought you back to me. My lover,
my husband, my heart's dearest, try to
remember ! "

" I remember nothing," he said. " This
is the madness of a strange wild dream.
Presently I shall wake and find myself
lying on golden bracken, while the dawn
breaks in the east, and the stars pale in the
sky. I have dreamed this dream before. I
shall wake. It will mean losing you; but I
must wake." He leapt to his feet and
shouted the last words ; " I *must* wake ! "

"Hush, my dearest, hush!" She spoke as if soothing a startled child. "Sit down, and I will explain. I can make it all clear if you will listen patiently. To you it is startling. But I have waited so long; I have known so long that you were coming. Sit down and listen. Striding about the room will not wake you, because this is no dream. It is blessed, blessed reality. Listen, Nigel! Listen, belovèd! I will make it all quite clear."

She rose, poured out a glass of wine and brought it to him.

"Drink this. How your hand shakes!... No; I will not touch you; but I beg of you to drink it."

She crossed the room, unlocked a bureau, took from it a despatch-box and placed it beside her on the couch.

"Now help me to tell you by listening calmly.

"We had three years of most perfect married life. No woman ever had such a lover, such a husband, as you were to me.

No man was ever so adored by his wife as you were by me. We were old enough to understand our happiness and to take it to the full. I was twenty-eight and you were thirty when I lost you; but you were so gloriously young, so full of life and love and laughter. I used to say you would never grow up. Sometimes I felt like wife and mother in one, my heart overflowing with the tenderness of both. Yet you were so wise and strong and grandly good. In all things spiritual and mental I leaned on you and learned of you.

"We had one little daughter, a year old on that fatal 12th of August; but, dear though she was to us both, you were my All. My whole body and soul were yours, wrapped up in you. And your love for me was such a sweet deep mystery of tenderness that I scarce dared think of it, save when you were near me. Surely it is given to few to love as we loved, to experience what we experienced.

"We lived much in the open; riding,

walking, climbing together. You were a magnificent swimmer and loved the sea. Often at dawn on a summer morning, you would leave our bed, dash down to the shore, and swim up the golden pathway, straight towards the rising sun.

"Our room is over this one. Our windows open on to a broad balcony running along the top of the veranda. There a powerful telescope is mounted.

"My heart always failed me over these early swims. You were so far from the shore, out in the ocean; no possible help at hand. I used to watch you through the telescope, and, knowing this, you would turn and smile and wave to me and speak my name. Often you dived into the bottomless deep of waters. Then your anxious wife could see nothing but an expanse of sky and ocean. After what seemed an hour of suspense, you would reappear in the sparkling ripples, laughing, shaking the salt water from your eyes, and bounding along with the strength and grace of a splendid sea-lion. Then I would breathe again and slip back to bed as you neared the shore and I lost you under the lee of the cliffs.

" But when you came back to my arms, I used to hold you close to my beating heart and say : 'Oh, Nigel, my dearest ! Some day those treacherous waters will swallow you up, and you will come back to me no more.'

" ' I shall always come back to you, my sweet,' you would make answer. ' If I lay fifty fathoms deep, and *you* called, I should hear and come back.'

" Then you would quite suddenly fall asleep ; but I would keep vigil, praying Heaven that you might never lie fifty fathoms deep, and loving the salt on my lips, as I softly kissed your damp hair.

" Nigel, do you remember ? "

The man in the chair put out his hand, groping blindly for the glass, and moistened his lips before he made answer.

" I remember nothing," he said.

" One lovely August evening we sat together on the shore. It was our baby's birthday. She was a year old. It had been a happy, merry day. We had been up to the nursery, where, surrounded by soft, furry toys, she slept. We stood together on either side of her crib, looking down at the rose-petal face with its aureola of tumbled golden hair.

"'Nothing of the Italian there,' you remarked. Your dark colouring and vivid vitality came from an Italian grandfather on your mother's side, from whom you also took your second name.

"'I want a little Guido, some day,' I whispered, as we turned away.

"'All in good time,' you answered, laughing softly, and slipped your arm through mine.

"We strolled down to the beach and watched a blood-red sunset.

"A sudden wind arose, gusty and fitful, blowing countless little white caps across the bay.

"A French woman, who, with her two daughters, had taken a hunting lodge near

by for the season, joined us on the beach.
We found them pleasant neighbours, viva-
cious and amusing. Madame de Villebois
had walked along the shore. '*Mes filles*'
were out sailing, in their little '*barquette à
voile*.' Presently it leapt into view, rounding
the point; a pretty picture in the sunset
glow.

"Seated upon the rocks just below this
cliff, we watched the tiny skiff dancing and
curtseying toward the middle of our bay.

"'Gusty for sailing,' you remarked; and
the next moment we could see that they
were in difficulties. The sails flapped loose,
then bellied suddenly, and the boat lurched.

"'Oh, Sir Nigel,' cried madame, with
clasped hands, 'bring out your rowing boat
and go to help them!'

"'I'm awfully sorry,' you said; 'but the
boat is under repairs.'

"At that instant the sail belched again;
the girls stood up; the skiff heeled over,
and they were flung into the water.

"Then followed a pandemonium of

screaming. Madame shrieked, and flew to the water's edge, crying : ' Sir Nigel, save them ! Save them ! *Oh, mon Dieu ! Mes enfants !* '

" The girls screamed in the water, catching at the bottom of the upturned boat. They could swim enough just to keep their heads above water. Their shrieks of terror were appalling.

" You flung off your coat and dashed down the beach in your flannels.

" ' Keep madame out of the sea, darling,' you shouted out to me, as I ran behind you. ' I will bring the girls in one at a time.'

" I put my arms round the frantic mother, and we stood together watching you.

" Even in such a moment, my heart thrilled at the sight of your magnificent swimming, as you forged through the waves at almost incredible speed. It did not occur to me to be afraid. Often, when I had misjudged my strength or been caught by the current, you had brought me safely to shore, swimming on your back with one arm

around me, while I lay on your chest in
perfect security, hearing your voice close to
my ear, saying : 'All right, my darling !
We can't sink.   Breathe, and rest, and trust
yourself to me.'   These slim French girls
would be nothing compared with my height
and weight.

" ' He will save them easily, madame,' I
said. ' Keep calm.   He will bring them in,
one at a time.'

" The frantic screams of the girls became
more ear-piercing.   I had never heard a
sound so appalling.

" ' Hold on ! ' you shouted. ' Hold on !
I am coming !   Hold on ! '

" Just before you reached them, one lost
her grip of the boat ; it slipped away from
her clinging fingers, and, turning, she swam
and struggled towards you.   In an instant
you had her by the arm, holding her
up.

" I remember wondering why she did
not cease screaming.   You were evidently

reasoning with her and trying to draw her on to your chest.

"At that moment the other girl left the boat, swam up behind you, and clasped you frantically round the throat.

"You let go of the first, in order to seize those throttling fingers; but she caught at your wrists and held them.

"Instantly you all went under, in a churning mass; then came to the surface— you fighting desperately—only to disappear again.

"Then, for one instant I saw a brown hand appear, pointing heavenward; a girl's white fingers locked around the wrist.

"Then that also vanished, and nothing remained, but the boat, drifting bottom upwards, and the fainting French woman in my arms.

"My Man, my Life, my All, lay drowning fathoms deep in the treacherous, cruel sea, while I stood helpless on the shore.

· · · · ·

" When the precious body was recovered a week later, those gripping fingers had to be cut from throat and wrists, that it might lie alone in the graveyard on the hill. I was not allowed to see It; so my last memory of my Darling was that vision of him in his glorious strength, as he swam through the waters, with no thought of personal danger, shouting to the drowning girls: 'Hold on! I am coming!'

" And, when the chill waters of my own despair threatened to engulf me, I seemed to hear again those ringing tones: 'Hold on! I AM COMING!'

" Then something happened which gave them a new meaning, and awakened in my own mind a train of thought which surely saved my reason.

" Your will was found, leaving all you possessed to me, and with it a letter addressed: '*To my wife; for her eye alone.*'

" I had been so haunted by the remembrance of that right hand, pointing skyward from the sea, and now I was to receive a message, penned by those precious fingers, which should indeed point out a ray of hope in the black sky of my sunless future.

" Nigel, do you remember ? "

The man in the chair slipped his brown hands into the pockets of his coat. He did not lift his eyes from the floor.

" I remember nothing," he said, very low.

" Then I must shew you your letter, which no eye save my own has ever seen."

She unlocked the despatch-box, took from it a small jewel-case, opened this with a gold key hanging from a chain around her wrist ; then, from a sealed envelope drew some half-dozen sheets of closely written manuscript. Leaning forward, she held them toward him.

Slowly, with evident reluctance, the lean brown hand came out of the coat pocket.

He took them from her, and let his eyes rest on the first page.

D

There followed moments of tense silence.

The tall clock, in the corner of the room, ticked loudly.

Out seaward, a nightbird screeched.

An owl in the fir wood behind the house, hooted thrice.

The fire fell together, and shot up tongues of flame.

At last he lifted hunted eyes to her face.

"It is my handwriting," he said, "or something very like it. But it is dated August 12th, 1882, thirteen months before my birth."

"Read it," said Lady Tintagel.

"I cannot."

"You must."

She rose, placed a shaded electric lamp on the table at his elbow; then switched off all other lights.

Seated in the shadow on the couch, she watched the dark face, so fine in its stern intentness, bending over the paper; the strong, nervous hand waiting to turn each

page; the dark hair, from which no crop-
ping could cut the curl.

"God in heaven," she sighed, "he has
come back to me in answer to the insistence of my frantic prayer; but he has
returned emptied of all memory. Oh, of
Thine infinite mercy, let there rise in his
mind the floodtide of remembrance."

Thus she prayed and yearned and hoped,
while the man in the chair slowly read the
letter, written, in his own handwriting, a
year before his birth.

"*August* 12*th*, 1882.

"MY OWN SWEET WIFE,

"You and I are so full of happy, buoyant
life, that it seems a strange anomaly that I
should sit down to write to you of death:
we are so intimately one in heart and mind,
so wedded in each moment of our perfect
life together, that there seems no need to
face the possibility of parting. Yet, lately,
there has come to me a chill presentiment
that, in the very middle of life and joy, a

sudden death may come with one swift
stroke ; that you and I, belovèd, counting
on fifty blissful years together, may, in one
fatal moment, be wrenched apart.

" So I have made my will, leaving everything to you. All is in order. Fergusson
will manage the estate. Thomas and his
wife can be wholly trusted in the house. I
leave my wife in faithful hands.

" So much for outward things. But what
can I say to comfort you, my Love, my
Own, in the utter loneliness of heart and
soul, which will, alas, be yours when you
read this ?

" Try to realise that we are not lost to
one another.

> " ' Nothing can untwine
> Thy life from mine.'

" We are eternally one, belovèd. Time is
made up of uncertainties ; not so Eternity.
' *Lord, Thou hast been our Dwelling Place
in all generations.*' When we pass out of
Time, we just go home again to that safe

Dwelling Place.   We are so safe in Eternity.

"And our love, yours and mine, being eternal we shall find one another again. Don't think of me as dead. Think of me as more vividly alive than ever ; yours still ; always wholly, utterly yours.

" But my belovèd, however hard you find it to bear the sudden silence, however much you long for just one word, one sign—never turn to a spiritualistic medium, or to spirit- ualism in any form.   I hold that thing to be a most damnable device of the Devil's for bamboozling the minds of men ; leading stricken hearts to believe they are holding converse with their Dead, when, in reality, demons intervene and whisper foolish nothings, till they trap the soul, confuse the mind, and wreck the moral and spiritual life. *Better a holy silence, than a lying whisper.* Better a parting bravely borne in faith and patience, than an attempt to bridge the chasm by forbidden means.

" Yet we *may* meet again on earth, if it be God's will for us, before we spend our great Eternity together. We have often talked of this. You know how firmly we believe that we have met before, in other times, in other climes; that we have lived and loved, striven together, risen together to God's great purposes of fresh development. We may yet meet again in Time; find each other, know each other; ' rise, on stepping-stones of our dead selves, to higher things.' Many adventures into Time may be necessary to our full completion for Eternity. Remember all we have said of this subject, and do not think of Death as the end. It is but passing on to fuller life, to fresh beginnings, to great opportunities.

" Of course we must bear in mind that all this is necessarily speculative. We cannot dogmatise upon uncertainties. Ideas of our own concerning the future state can be but theoretical. The only certainties are to be found in Divine revelation, and our theories, if they are worth anything, will harmonise with the Word of God.

"However, two great certainties I leave you to cling to in your loneliness:—Our eternal Dwelling Place is in the love of God; and our own perfect love remains to us eternally. Wherever I may be while you read this, I am loving you still, with my whole being; I am all your own, and I hold you mine for ever.

"Now I will lock away this letter with my will and other papers. Please God, it may be fifty years before your dear eyes rest upon it. The fact that I have written it, lifts me from the dull weight of vague apprehension.

"As I sit writing in the Oak Room, you lie in our chamber overhead, with our little one in your arms. Your precious life has been spared, and a new life has been given. Heaviness endured for a night, but joy came in the morning. You have come safely through this dreaded ordeal. Why should I apprehend an unknown danger?

"So I will put away all apprehension

with this letter, and go up to the radiance
of your smile and the glad certainty which
is mine when I clasp you closely in my
arms, my wife, my own !

" Your lover and your husband, in Time
and in Eternity,   " NIGEL TINTAGEL."

He folded the many sheets and returned
them to the envelope.

A strange calm had entered into his soul,
a quiet strength which seemed to say :
" Knowing so much, I must know more ; I
must know all."

He ceased to feel hunted and haunted.
He had been brought face to face, in these
pages, with a great love ; whether his own
or another's seemed at that moment
scarcely to matter. The very knowledge
of such a love lifted him to a higher
plane. Luke Sparrow had seen deep into
the most sacred recesses of the heart of
Nigel Tintagel. His own empty heart
received this as a trust. A patient strength
replaced his restive horror of resentment

at a situation so utterly beyond all human understanding.

He laid the letter on the table beside him, switched off the light, turned his chair so that he looked into the fire, and did not face the woman on the couch, and said, very gently : " What happened next ? "

" Nigel," she said : " Do you remember ? "

" I remember nothing," he answered ; but the harshness was gone from his voice : its tone was infinitely sad and tender. " I remember nothing. But I am ready to listen. I want you to tell me all. I will try to understand. You need not fear any wild outbursts now. For the sake of what you believe—whether it be true or not—I would give my life to bring you comfort. Tell me all."

The firelight flickered on the tragic face. She saw a look of peace it had not held before. She saw a faint suggestion of the look of youth which, in its appeal to her tenderness, had made the man she loved so adorable.

"Oh, Nigel," she whispered; "Nigel, belovèd!"

"What happened next?"

"I read your letter many times. Your arms seemed to steal around me as I read. I turned my face against your breast, and wept myself to calmness. It mattered not that my head was buried in my pillow. Your letter had brought you so near; you came between me and all outward things. I repeated again and again: 'Nothing can untwine my life from thine.'

"The warning against spiritualism reached me just in time. The poor French 'Madame' was an ardent spiritualist. She had secured a medium, and was already in communication with her daughters. They had told her their favourite flowers and had reminded her that they used to prefer 'Chocolat' to 'café au lait,' for breakfast. Also that 'Antoinette' used to darn their stockings. Antoinette was an old 'bonne' who had been with them many years.

"These undeniable facts filled 'Madame'

with a holy rapture. She implored me to come and receive like comfort. I might have yielded, had it not been for your timely warning.

"Madame's husband, sons, another daughter and two cousins, had come to her in her sorrow. She was quickly growing resigned—comforted—almost elated. Her 'deuil' was infinitely becoming.

"But I? I had been robbed of my All. I dreaded Madame de Villebois' frequent visits, yet knew my darling would not wish me to refuse to see her, lest she should think I resented the awful part her children had played in my life's tragedy. And after all, it was Madame's outpourings which first caused the Great Idea to formulate in my mind.

"'Ah,' she cried one day, 'the brave, the wonderful Sir Nigel! So full of "*joie de vivre*"! So life abounding! No; he cannot stay *parmi les morts*. Such as he, must live again. . . . Quite soon, quite soon, he will live again. *Il reviendra!*'

" ' Quite soon ?   Quite soon ? '   I repeated
the words, when my visitor had departed.
Quite soon !   Ah, what would it be to know
that my darling was on earth again ;
breathing the same air ; seeing the same
sunshine. Oh, if he came back *quite soon !*

" I remembered all you had thought and
said on this great subject. You took the
Bible instance of the prophet Elijah reappearing in John the Baptist—' *More* than a
prophet ' because a prophet twice born—as
giving important data from which to draw
conclusions.

" Christ Himself had said, in unmistakable
language : ' If ye will receive it, this *is*
Elijah which was for to come. . . . *And
they knew him not*, but have done unto
him whatsoever they listed.' These clear
statements, you said, swept away all
possibility of explaining John the Baptist as
a mere type of Elijah. He was, without
doubt, a reincarnation of the great prophet
of fire. Elijah caught away on the banks
of the river Jordan, his mission incomplete,

reappearing on the same spot more than eight centuries later, to continue his work of ' turning the hearts of the disobedient to the wisdom of the just.'

"It would take too long were I to endeavour to remind you of the perfect working out of every detail in the wonderful, inspired story—the comparatively slight stress laid upon the preparation of the little earthly body, miraculous though it was; the thirty years of silence and mystery in the deserts; then the triumphant heralding of the full-grown prophet : ' There was a man, *sent from God*, whose name was John ': his very appearance exactly corresponding to the Old Testament descriptions of Elijah.

"You held that, though the actual physical body of a child is prepared by his parents, according to nature's laws, his spirit—his *ego*—comes direct from God, entering the body at the moment of birth, with the first independent breath the baby draws. ' God breathed into his nostrils the breath of life ; and man became a living soul.' This followed the forming of the body. 'Then shall the dust return to the earth as it was : and the spirit shall return unto God Who gave it.' You cannot *return* to a place, unless you have been there before.

"From this you argued that, though a certain amount of likeness to the parents might be inherited, the *ego*, being the essential part, would mould the body into the appearance it had worn before. A strongly developed spirit, rich with many former experiences, would probably stamp its own likeness so strongly on the bodily development that very little resemblance to the immediate parents would obtain. This is why, in brilliant, gifted children we see so little family likeness ; whereas in families in which all are as alike as peas in a pod, you find a lack of gifts, a poverty of mental development, a want of originality, which point to no previous experiences. Having no individual *ego* of its own, the newly created spirit in its first existence, allows the body to become an exact copy of its parents. 'Adam begat a son in his own likeness, after his image.'

"With all reverence, you regarded the incarnation of our Blessed Lord as throwing important light upon this point. From all eternity He had had an outward form. Man was created in His image. He was the pattern from which man was fashioned. In Old Testament records we find that He appeared many times upon earth and was seen of men : to Adam, to Abraham, to Joshua, to Gideon, to Manoah, to Daniel. These all knew Him, as we say in human parlance, by sight. The hosts of heaven knew Him and adored Him in His divinely glorious outward form. Now comes the time when He is to lay aside that glory and be born, very man, of the substance of an earthly mother. The little body, stainless and sinless, is prepared of a pure virgin through the operation of the Holy Ghost. 'A body hast Thou prepared for

me.' At the moment of its birth, the great
ego of the Son of God enters into it. Then
'When He bringeth in the first begotten
into the world, He saith, And let all the
angels of God worship Him '—the scene on
Bethlehem's hills. By degrees that body
grows, moulded by the *ego* within, into the
perfect likeness of what a body must ever
be, indwelt by the great *Ego*—the Son of
God. He is seen by angels, and recognised.
He is seen by demons, and recognised.
He is seen by Moses and Elijah on the
holy mount and, undoubtedly, recognised.
Then—the work of redemption accomplished—raised from the grave and glorified, He takes that same body, bearing the
actual scars of crucifixion, back into the
Heavens. Would their King return to
them in wholly different guise ?

"No; the *ego*, in its changeless consis-
tency, has done its perfect work. Whether
'in the beginning, with God,' or born of
the Virgin Mary in Bethlehem's stable, or
ascending triumphant 'far above all princi-

pality, and power, and might, and domi-
nion, and every name that is named, not
only in this world but also in that which
is to come '—He is, in outward appearance,
as well as in nature and character, Jesus
Christ, the same yesterday, to-day, and
for ever.

" From these sacred facts you deduced
that any reincarnation of a fully developed
ego would probably reproduce again the
likeness to its previous bodily appearance,
modified to a certain extent by a diversity
of parents, less or more, according to the
strength and richness of the *ego*.

" From this it follows that if one lived
who still held the conscious recollection of
a person in one incarnation, and if a second
incarnation followed so quickly that a meeting on this earth could take place between
the newly-arrived and the one who remembered, there would probably be recognition
on the part of the latter.

" You also believed that the handwriting,
with certain modifications, would be the

same ; handwriting being so closely allied to character, when allowed free development.

" You believed that the sub-conscious mind is an eternal thing, and holds stored within it every detail of every episode in every incarnation, be they many or few. But the conscious mind and memory, being dependent upon the growth and development of the actual physical brain, knows and remembers the happenings of that body's life, only. The sub-conscious mind cannot be drawn upon consciously ; but sometimes there springs up from it, into the conscious mind, a haunting memory of previous existence : ' I have been there before ! I have done this before ! '

" Love being so largely a matter of the sub-consciousness, lovers are quick to find and to recognise one another, when they meet again reincarnate. This accounts for the sudden instinctive attraction known as ' love at first sight.' It is, in reality, two faithful lovers hailing one another with joy and delight by the unconscious means of the sub-conscious memory. After marriage this sub-conscious memory may become an exquisite certainty, adding a richness to the bliss of newly-wedded love.

" Great gifts can also be handed up to the new body from the sub-conscious *ego*. A born musician is one who, having become a great musician before by means of long study and practice, is re-born rich in the possession of the gift of musical expression. A born orator has been a practised speaker in a former life, and now, without knowing that he does so, draws freely on his sub-consciousness for inspiration.

" *Genius* is the natural intellect so attuned to the sub-conscious mind that its fount of inspiration flows through it unhindered.

" *Madness* is the sub-conscious mind gaining undue control, bursting the dams of reason and restraint, and carrying all before it into mental chaos. A writer who, discovering that he can do more vividly imaginative work when his sub-consciousness is in the ascendancy, puts himself under the influence of drugs in order to obtain this mental condition, may, for a time, produce work which will astonish the world ; but, before long, there will come the inevitable fiasco—loss of will power, loss of mental and moral perspective ; nerve and brain irritation ; insanity !

"Ah, how crudely and disjointedly I am repeating all this ! It was your favourite subject, and I might give you essays of your own to read, with chapter and verse, and carefully worked out illustration. I have them all here. I almost know them by heart. But this hurried outline must serve to remind us of all you held and believed.

"Well—to take up the thread of the happenings of those sad days—first, your letter ; secondly, Madame de Villebois' remark ; thirdly, my recollection of all you had taught and told me, awakened in me the passionate desire that your rebirth into the world should take place at once.

In my awful loss and loneliness it seemed to me that such unspeakable comfort would come from the knowledge that my belovèd was actually on earth again; even if, at first, he were but a little helpless babe.

" I had always loved the photographs of my baby Nigel so tenderly—I seemed to have known and loved you at every age. At times I saw each age in you and adored it as I saw it.

" And the years would pass, and you would grow up. After all, when you were a man of twenty, I should only be forty-eight. We should certainly have found each other by then, and my darling would know me, and would not think me old, for had he not written: 'Wherever I may be I am loving you still, with my whole being. I am all your own, and I hold you mine for ever. . . . We *may* meet again on earth, if it be God's will for us.' I knew you meant by this, a fresh incarnation for both; but I could not see why I must wait during long, lonely years, or why death must come first.

"I began to pray with desperate, frantic energy that my darling might come back without delay.

"A wild, sweet joy and comfort came to soothe my agony.

"I walked along the shore and prayed aloud. I roamed the moors in paroxysms of petition. I prayed all night. I thought of the many little bodies there must be, prepared and ready, just waiting for a splendid, eager spirit to enter them at the moment of birth. Could not my darling be sent to one of these and, growing up in it to his full beauty and stature, come and find his wife again?

"At last, one night, I remembered that morning when you came in from a swim at sunrise, when I had been so fearful for your safety, and how I had said: 'Oh, Nigel, my dearest! Some day those treacherous waters will swallow you up, and you will come back to me no more.' But you, lying in my arms, had made answer: 'I shall always come back to you, my sweet.

If I lay fifty fathoms deep and *you* called,
I should hear and come back.'

"I remembered this, just before midnight,
on the 11th of September.

"I had begun to feel as if all my prayers
and pleadings with heaven had been useless,
had failed to obtain any response.

"Now, I would take my husband at his
word, and call him—call him—call him!

"I slipped from my bed, opened the
French window and went out on to the
balcony.

"There stood the telescope through which
I used to watch you while you swam!

"A high wind blew, warm but boisterous.

"The sea roared and pounded against the
rocks at the base of the cliff.

"I stood in the wind-swept darkness and
lifted my eyes to the distant stars.

"'Nigel!' I called aloud: 'Oh, Nigel,
my lover, my husband, come back to earth!
Come out of Eternity, back into Time. I
cannot *live* on this earth without you. You
promised—you *promised* to come from fifty

fathoms deep, if I called. NIGEL ! COME !
Ask to be born once more. Then grow up
quickly, and seek, and seek, and seek,
belovèd, until you find me. Nigel, your
own wife calls ! Oh, Nigel ! COME ! '

"Long I stood with clasped hands,
gazing upward to the stars.

"The wind moaned and shrieked through
the pines. The sea roared in the distance.
Behind the house, an owl hooted, like a lost
soul in agony, and seemed to mock my
prayer.

"Up on the hill, the church bell tolled
thrice.

"Suddenly an intense drowsiness overcame me—I, who for a month past had
scarcely slept. I crept back to bed and fell
asleep as my head touched the pillow.

"I slept until ten o'clock the next
morning, then woke with such a sense of
comfort and joy, that I could not understand
what had happened.

"Then I remembered my call to you at
midnight. And then I knew—knew with

an unhesitating certainty—that my belovèd had kept his word; that some time between midnight and ten o'clock, on this 12th of September, 1883, he had come back, for my sake, and was now on earth once more, spending his first day as a little living, growing, beautiful man-child.

"Oh, the wonder of those hours! My breasts thrilled and ached with joy and longing. Ah, if I could but press his baby lips against them! The wife in me was merged in the wish that I could be his mother! I lived again. I smiled and laughed. For a long, weary month I had trailed about. I now ran up and down stairs. I lifted my arms to the sun and blessed him, as he rose in the heavens, because he was shining on my little boy. I tried to picture his nursery, his bassinet, his little gowns and flannels.

"My household evidently thought me demented; but I knew that this joy had saved my reason.

"During the next few days I scanned

with eager eyes the births column in the 'Times,' making a list of the names and addresses of all the parents who had had sons on the 12th of September.

"Oh, Nigel, Nigel! I little thought—a doorstep! A deserted bundle! A Foundlings' Institution! Oh, my dear, if I could have flown to that doorstep and found you, and brought you home! But—did you not say there was a date on the label, the date of your birth, written beneath 'Returned Empty'?"

"Yes," he said. "You shall see the label. There is a date."

He drew his chair near to the couch, so that he could reach her hands with his own. He took the label from his pocket-book, and laid it upon her lap. She lifted it and, bending towards him, read it by the firelight.

RETURNED EMPTY

September 12th, 1883.

" Oh, Nigel," she said, " the day—the very day ! "

" I know," he answered. " I was listening for it as you talked. I felt it would come."

" And it is to-day," she said. " To-day ! This is your thirtieth birthday."

He looked at her with a wistful smile ; a smile of such pathetic melancholy that it chilled her heart.

" It is," he said. " And nobody in the world knows it, save you and I."

She stretched out her hands.

He took them in his and held them firmly. They looked into each other's eyes in silence.

" Speak to me," she whispered.

" Not yet," he said. " You have more to tell. And it has always been my way to think long and steadily, and then to speak —and to speak to the point. You and I are facing an awful mystery ; but at least we are facing it together."

Suddenly she felt herself before a judgment-seat.

"Oh, Nigel," she whispered, "I am afraid."

"You need not be," he answered, and bending laid his lips upon her hand. "I have read Nigel Tintagel's letter."

"And do you remember?"

"I remember nothing. But my soul is slowly struggling up into the light. After long years in outer darkness, at last I am finding the way home to God."

Again he laid his lips upon her hands; but they were cold as death, and her heart trembled.

"Tell me the rest," he said.

She steadied her voice with an effort.

"There is not much to tell. It has been a long, long time of seeking and waiting. I kept count of each year. I made little clothes of the right size, and gave them away. In the summers I went from one seaside place to another and roamed about the shore, seeking among the little boys who shouted and played, rode donkeys, wielded their wooden spades, and made sand castles. I neglected my little daughter because I wanted only the boy who was doubly my own. Then I remembered she was yours, and flew back to make amends.

"When the right time came, I went to the public schools, Eton, Harrow, Marlborough, Rugby. I watched the sports; I saw the prize-givings. Crowds of fine British lads were there; but the face I sought was not among them.

"Later, I went to Oxford and Cambridge. I saw degrees conferred; I viewed the races. I went to Lord's; you had been keen on cricket. But you were not there.

"At last I knew your education must be over. You must have taken your place in the world—a man among men. Then I gave up my search, and waited here—just waited. Your room was always ready. I felt certain you would come to me at last.

"Eight years ago our daughter married.

Then I was left alone, and I was glad. Little Nigel was born, and he was *so* like you. But that was no comfort to me ; it was you I wanted, not a likeness. I never doubted that you would find me at last.

"And to-night—to-night, after thirty years—I looked up and saw my husband's eyes gazing in at me through the window.

"The very greatness of the moment kept me calm. I had just to make sure you would not go. I could not tell Colin and Eva ; they would have thought me mad. But old Thomas knew. He recognised you at once."

"Recognised me ? "

"Yes, Nigel. He had known and loved and served you from boyhood. He ran beside your pony the first time you rode alone. He and his wife are the only people left among the household who remember you. When I sent him to fetch you in, I told him you had come at last, and warned him to give no sign of recognition until I had found out how much you knew.

He has shared with me the long years of vigil."

Luke Sparrow buried his face in his hands.

"Good God," he muttered; "let me keep my reason."

Midnight sounded slowly from a distant belfry.

The old clock in the corner whirred its warning, and struck the hour.

Lady Tintagel took up her jewel-case.

"Come and sit here beside me, and see why Thomas could not fail to know you."

He rose. His knees shook. He felt queer and dizzy. It had been a long time of mental strain.

Lady Tintagel turned on a light behind her, and moved the despatch-box.

He took his seat beside her on the couch.

A packet of faded photographs were in her hands.

"This is your first. Your mother gave it to me; my baby Nigel; six months old. She used to call you her little Black Prince because of your dark eyes and regal bearing."

He took the faded picture and bent over it.

The bright eyes of the baby had survived the yellowing process of sixty years. They held a look of baby omniscience as they stared into the haunted eyes of the man who bent and looked. The little figure sat erect, one finger lifted as if solemnly pointing a moral. The mother, on whose lap the baby sat, was so much absorbed in watching its expression, that her back was turned. He could only see a gracious figure and smoothly braided hair.

"Aged three," said Lady Tintagel, passing another.

The same bright eyes, now merry with childish laughter, and half hidden in a mass of tumbled curls. Bare legs, white socks, strap shoes, a wooden horse. The marvel was that he stayed still ten seconds to be photographed. He must have whooped and run, the moment it was over.

"Aged seven," said Lady Tintagel. "I love him in his kilt."

A graceful little figure, in full Highland dress; standing, as if just arrested in a dance, one hand above his head; his dark eyes shining, his curls escaping from the Glengarry bonnet.

The man's hand shook as he laid it down.

"No more just now," he said, thickly. "I don't see—very clearly."

"Just the last," she insisted, "the last of all; that you may understand how it was that Thomas knew you."

She drew out a cabinet portrait and placed it in his hands. Beneath it was written: "*Nigel, one week before I lost him. August*, 1883."

A man in flannels, carrying a pair of sculls over his shoulder; smiling that he should be caught by a photographer on his way to the boats; his whole face and figure radiating health and happiness: a look of well-being, of honest, genial love to all

E

mankind; of innate goodness, purity, strength—a man made for love and for companionship; a man to whom a woman would trust herself, body and soul, and never regret it.

No contrast could have been more marked than that between the man portrayed and the man who now looked at the portrait; but the contrast was one of heart, mind, character, not of outward semblance. For, as he looked, seeing only the portrait, in a room growing suddenly black, he knew he looked upon himself— himself, as he might have been; himself, as he once was.

Lady Tintagel returned the others to their place of safety. She fitted them all in with loving care; then turned to take the last.

"Can you wonder——" she began : then paused, dismayed.

The man beside her tried to rise, groped blindly for support, then swayed slowly forward, and fell senseless at her feet.

SCENE VIII

The Dawn Breaks

Scene VIII

THE DAWN BREAKS

WHEN consciousness returned, he found himself stretched at full length upon the couch.

Lady Tintagel knelt beside him, her arms around him.

He could feel the rapid beating of her heart; her soft, quick breathing, mingled with kisses, on his brow and hair. Words of tenderness unthinkable poured from her lips.

He woke at once to vivid consciousness; but lay with eyes closed, waiting till he could gather up his strength, master himself, and take hold on calm speech.

And all the while her flood of tenderness poured over him. It was as if his helplessness had broken down all barriers, his loss of consciousness had burst the

bonds of her reserve. The love and longing of those thirty years throbbed in her
clasping arms.

"My Love, my own! Don't go from me
again. Ah, when you wake you will remember all! Nigel, you will remember."

She held him closer to her breast. He
felt the desperate strength in those poor
clinging arms.

"Dear God, when he awakes he will
remember! He will call his own wife by
her name. He will know all at last. At
last he will remember."

Her tears and kisses rained upon his
face.

At length he spoke.

"Loose me," he said.

"Mine," she murmured, her trembling
lips against his hair. "Mine again, at last.
I have waited so long—so long."

He shrank away from her.

"Loose me," he said, "loose me and let
me go. I do not want to hurt you."

"You could not hurt me, Nigel. I am

past being hurt. My love would welcome pain." Yet her lips quivered. Her eyes searched his. No answering light of love was in their sombre depths.

"You would loose me at once," he said, "if you could know how much I loathe that you should hold and touch me."

Her arms fell away from him. She pressed her hands against her breasts, as if his words had been an actual blow. She recoiled from him, moving backwards on her knees, gazing at him in dumb dismay; then hid her stricken face in both her hands.

He sprang to his feet, crossed to the window, and flung aside a curtain.

Dawn was breaking in one pale silver streak on the horizon.

Sea birds called to one another in the distance.

A chill mist lay on the lawns. In the corner of the veranda he could see the ghostly outline of the chair in which he had waited the night before.

He turned back into the lighted room.

The fire burned low. He stirred the embers and threw on fresh logs.

He raised Lady Tintagel from her knees and led her to the couch.

"Forgive me," he said. "How I hate to give you pain! But our only hope is to be absolutely honest with ourselves and with each other."

She lifted sorrowful eyes, but made no answer.

"Will you forgive me if that which I must say is hard to hear? It would help me if you could say: 'I will forgive you.'"

Her smile was sadder far than tears.

"We never forgave one another, Nigel. If need for forgiveness arose, love had already met it, and swept it away. Besides, I do not blame you for my pain. Say what you will."

He stood long silent, looking into the heart of the red embers.

At last he spoke.

"It is dangerous work," he said, "to

tamper with the Dead. The Dead are safe
with God, at home in that eternal Dwelling
Place. Do you realise the awful wrong you
did to me and to yourself, by that insistent
call which brought me back? Through
all these years in the great Life beyond,
the fulness of my love would have been
yours. That letter told you of a changeless
tie—you mine, I yours, for ever. But it
also spoke of a parting bravely borne, in
faith and patience. A sorrow thus endured
would have kept us both safe in the Will
of God. But you called me back, with
passionate insistence, and—it seems—I
responded to the passion of that appeal, and
came. But in so doing I put myself outside
the supreme Will. Had I waited God's
time for my return to earthly life, I might
have come strong in His strength and
grace, filled with His Holy Spirit, ready to
overcome, to rise at His command to a
higher level than I had before attained.
Instead of which I am but a poor derelict,
shipwrecked upon life's ocean, drifting

rudderless at the mercy of each wind of circumstance. And alas, I returned empty —emptied of that Spark Divine, which is the very essence of the life of man ; emptied of aspiration ; emptied of the capacity for love. I have no assurance of the Love of God ; I have no remembrance of my love for you ; I have no power to feel love for others or to accept love offered me. For thirty wasted years I have been seeking, seeking, ever seeking, for earthly love, and now that I have found it, it is Dead Sea fruit—mere dust and ashes. I wander, God forsaken, like the demons of old, ' walking through dry places, seeking rest, and finding none.' I have no faith, I have no hope ; I ask only for Oblivion. ' Why hast thou disquieted me, to bring me up ? ' You who call yourself my loving wife ?

"One sentence in that letter which you say is my own, wakes in me a realisation of all that I have lost. ' Lord Thou hast been our Dwelling Place in all generations.' My soul remembers that divine security ;

but I have left it, and there is no return. You thought, while I lay senseless I should remember things of Time. Not so, but in a lightning flash of revelation I saw again Eternity."

Turning, he raised both arms, lifting his face with a light upon it which was not the dawn, nor any earthly light, but a pale reflection of the light of Heaven.

"God's Will!" he said. "When we go home to that great Dwelling Place, our holy passion is to do His Will. All earthly things—loves, hopes, desires—assume their right proportions. The one Essential is the great Will of God—that He in us, by us, through us, may in all things be glorified. All, in our earthly lives, which made for this, abides, and is ours still. All else is dross and cannot stand the fire—that purity of motive which is the very birthright of each immortal soul set free from earthly trammels of the flesh. To know His will and do it—this is Life Eternal; this is the joy supreme."

His arms dropped. The light faded from his countenance.

" I left it, at the call of earthly love. I stand before you empty, godless, damned."

" Nigel," she said ; " my heart is broken."

" I would I had a heart to break," he said.

The despair in her face left him cold. Yet still her faithful love caught at a straw of comfort.

" At least we are together in our misery."

" I am going," he said.

" Nigel ! You will not leave me ? "

" How can I stay ? A year younger than your own daughter, I cannot stand in my rightful place—nor would I, if I could."

" Nigel, stay as my son."

" How can I ? I am not your son, and I will not be a rich woman's protégé. I may have no capacity for love, but I have honour. I shall go, as I came, empty and alone. I will take nothing with me from this great house which you tell me is, in reality, my own."

"Nigel, there is one thing you *must* take with you. It was your tenderest gift to me. It has been so precious all these years; but now I have forfeited the right to wear it."

She drew her wedding-ring from her finger.

"I have failed you, utterly."

She held it out to him.

"The golden circlet, emblem of a love which is eternal, would mock me in my hopeless desolation. Take it, Nigel. It is all you can do for me. When you placed it on my finger, you had just said: 'Till death us do part'; and death has parted us."

"Not death," he said. "Life has parted us, not death."

A heavy sense of sorrow and compunction gripped him.

"Why do you ask me to do this? It leaves you neither wife nor widow."

" I *am* neither wife nor widow. I am not your widow, for you live. I am not your wife, for you loathe me, and are leaving me for ever."

" I do not loathe you," he said, in low, remorseful tones. " But you have shewn me what I was ; and you have made me what I am."

A spasm of deathly agony wrung her heart. Could he not spare her one cruel stab ?

She pressed the ring upon him.

" Take it, I implore you. And if ever the remembrance returns of all that this ring once meant to us, come back to me, and place it again upon my hand."

He took it. For what had it stood when last he held it in his hand ? The complete possession of a perfect love ?

He slipped it on to his little finger.

His gnawing misery grew. Why could he not say one word of kindness or of comfort to this stricken woman whose faithful heart was breaking ?

His hell was within him, "where the worm dieth not, and the fire is not quenched."

He rose abruptly. "I must go!" he said.

He crossed to the garden door and flung it wide.

A stream of golden sunshine poured in, paling the artificial light, and flooding the room with radiance.

The sun had risen, a great golden ball, above the sea, and was slowly ascending from the pearly mist on the horizon.

"I must go," he said, again; but a dreamy quality had come into his voice, and he leaned against the door post, gazing at the sunrise.

She came and stood beside him, and together they looked up to the rosy sky, flecked with soft billowy clouds of pearly whiteness, and down on the wide expanse of opal sea, reflecting in a royal highway from shore to horizon, the crimson glory of the rising sun.

The water seemed to shout, once more, in a silent chorus of sparkling voices: "This is the way to the City of Gold! Leap from the cliff! Take to the waters! This—and this only—is your road for Home."

Suddenly a look of hope shone in his eyes. His whole figure sprang to alertness. He was transformed.

"I must go!" he cried. "There lies the way." He pointed to the sparkling path upon the waters. "It is my only chance; my one way Home."

"Not that, Nigel! Oh, not that!" Her clinging hands caught at his coat. "You always said those who did that would lose——"

"Lose?" he shouted. "What have I to lose? Returned empty! I have nothing to lose."

He wrenched himself free from her detaining fingers. He gave no backward

glance. He sped across the lawn, like a
hound loosed from the leash ; leapt the iron
gate, and disappeared down the zigzag path
leading to the beach.

SCENE IX
The Watcher

Scene IX

THE WATCHER

LADY TINTAGEL turned back into the Oak Room, switched off the pale lights, gathered up her treasures, locked the despatch-box, and, taking it with her, crossed the hall and slowly mounted the stairs to her bedroom. Each step meant a separate effort. The mainspring of her life was broken. This was the end.

Arrived at her room, she slipped off her velvet gown, put on a soft white wrapper, and laid herself down upon the bed.

"'They went away toward the sunrising,'" she quoted. "Where is it written?" She repeated it, mechanically. "'They went away toward the sunrising.'"

Then memory returned and with it the shock of realisation.

He had gone. He had gone for ever.

He was swimming into the sunrise, and never coming back.

Dear God—was there no hope, no help ?

She rose from the bed.

She must watch to the end.

She went out on to the wide balcony, overlooking the sea, where stood the telescope.

SCENE X

"Turns Again Home"

"WHEN THAT WHICH DREW FROM OUT THE BOUNDLESS DEEP—TURNS AGAIN HOME"

WHEN Luke Sparrow reached the beach, he tore at his boot-laces, flung off his coat and, in less than twenty seconds, was swimming up the sunlit way, his eyes dazzled by the golden glory, his heart throbbing from his rapid race down the cliff.

He seemed to have burst invisible shackles which hitherto had held him captive.

"Free!" he shouted. "Free! On to the sunrise! No going back!"

Wild sea birds, flying above him, swooped and dipped, till their wings almost touched his face as they passed.

He laughed, and echoed their wild cries.

"God give me wings, that I may mount and rise!"

He dived into green depths where fishes flopped against his face, and waving arms of giant sea-weed tried to catch him as he passed.

He came to the surface gasping ; dashed the water from his eyes ; then settled into a steady breast-stroke, swimming out to sea, straight to the sun.

He swam. He swam. He swam. On, toward the shoreless horizon.

His heart pounded in his ears. Still he swam on.

His arms felt like lead. He folded them across his breast and swam without them.

His legs could move no more. He turned upon his back and lay, like a bit of driftwood, resting.

He grinned at the blue sky above him.

" Flotsam and jetson," he remarked confidentially to a swooping gull. " ' Returned Empty. This side up, with care.' That's more to the point just now. Don't peck at my eyes, you greedy brute ! Wait a week for that. . . . Here lies a poor derelict on the ocean of Time, at the mercy of every wind of circumstance. . . . Swim, you fool! Yonder lies your one way Home."

He turned over, and swam on and on, into the dazzling glory.

At length a dream-like sense of unreality came over him, a strange, sweet peace; a wish to fall asleep.

He heard church bells in the distance, growing nearer.

At first he thought they came floating out to sea from the land he had left behind, and he ceased swimming that he might listen.

Then they pealed louder, coming up—up —from the green depths beneath him.

Come down and find us!
Come down and find us!

He looked down and instantly sank— deep, deep, deep into the cool silence. Instinctively he held his breath, threw up his hands and rose to the surface; gasped, took a long breath; raised his arms above his head and went down like a stone.

Deeper, deeper, deeper.

The church bells pealed so loudly, he thought their clanging clamour would burst the drums of his ears.

> *They lose their immortality*
> *They lose their immortality*
> *Those who do this*
> *Those who do this*
> *Those who do this*
> *Those who do this*
> *They lose their immortality*

He was entangled in flapping sea-weed, but he fought himself free. It was very dark.

He threw up his arms and rose slowly to the surface.

The sun seemed miles above him, a pale phantom, luminous through the green waters.

It grew brighter. He reached the surface. It blazed upon him.

The church bells stopped suddenly. Everything stopped. His heart stopped. There was a great silence.

He was too tired to breathe. He clasped

his hands, lifted them slowly above his head, and went down for the third time.

As he sank he heard the head-master say : " Luke Sparrow—first prize " ; he saw the glitter of the Mayor's grand chain. All his school life rushed backward through his mind, and then—he was flinging down a rattle on the nursery floor, and the matron's voice was saying : " Poor little ' Returned Empty.' He won't even play with his rattle."

" I'm really drowning now," he thought. " The fools are right. This is my past life."

" *What does he want ?* " said the matron's voice. " *Who is he calling ?* "

Then—something burst in his brain, and in flaming letters of living fire a name illumined the icy blackness.

" MIRIAM ! My wife ! Miriam, my love, my life ! Good God, I can't leave her ! . . . Miriam, I'm coming ! Hold on, I am coming ! "

The weeds had him this time, but he fought like a madman.

" Miriam ! Belovèd ! "

His lungs were bursting, but he kept
out the water. Tons weight pressed down
his hands, but he lifted them.

" Miriam, my Love, I am coming ! "

The sun reappeared, a pale disc—no, by
God ! A dead face !

He was caught again. Sea-weed ? No ;
white hands, catching at his throat, throttling him. Curse them ! What matter
they while his wife waits. He fought
on.

" My Love, I am coming ! " He broke
free and rose—rose—rose.

The sun—Great God !—the air !

He breathed, choked, gasped, breathed
again ; lay on the surface, and panted. His
ribs seemed jammed upon his heart ; but,
as he breathed, they lifted. His lungs
expanded ; his sight cleared ; his heart beat
more steadily.

" Oh, belovèd ! Miriam ! Miriam ! Are
you there ? All else is a dream, save our
great love, my perfect, perfect mate."

Slowly he turned and looked toward the shore.

Far away, so far away; but he could see the line of cliffs and the house—his home and hers—standing clear against the fir woods. The upper windows seemed on fire, as they reflected the gold of the sunrise.

He measured the distance between himself and the shore. Could he swim it?

He started a slow breast-stroke, his eyes upon those flaming windows.

Then he remembered the telescope. He made out the balcony.

Dear God. Was she watching? Of course she was watching.

He fancied he could see a white figure.

He waved his arm and smiled. A glory of love was on his face.

"Miriam," he said, knowing the powerful lens brought him quite near and she would see him speak; "Miriam, you said I should remember all, if I remembered your name. And I do; oh, my belovèd, I do!"

As he swam the sunlight caught the wedding-ring—her wedding-ring—upon his finger. He missed a stroke to hold it up, then press it to his lips.

"I am coming, Sweet! I am coming!"

Then he swam on.

Love, surging through his soul, gave him strength.

The shore drew nearer. He could see her now, standing at the telescope.

"Miriam! Miriam!"

Her dear arms would be waiting. Her lips—her tenderness.

Could he last out? He swam feebly, but steadily.

As he neared the shore, a swiftly flowing current caught him. It held him stationary and his strength was ebbing.

One chance remained. He might win through under water. He took a deep breath, dived, and disappeared.

Swift, quick strokes—"Miriam! Miriam!" Desperate work; but for her dear sake!

He rose at last. He was through the

current and under the lee of the cliff. He could see the house no longer, but the zigzag path was there. His coat and his boots lay under the rocks.

He fought feebly with the water. His breath came in groans.

No; he could not do it, after all. Not another stroke. He must sink; he must give up, and sink.

He sank—and felt sand beneath his feet.

With a great cry he struggled through the water, reeled up the beach, and dropped like a log beside the rocks.

current, and under the lee of the cliff. He could see the house no longer, but the zigzag path was there. His coat and his boots lay under the rocks.

He fought feebly with the water. His breath came in groans.

No, he could not do it, after all. Not another stroke. He must sink; he must give up, and sink.

He sank—and felt sand beneath his feet. With a great cry he struggled through the water, reeled up the beach, and dropped like a log beside the rocks.

SCENE XI

"My Life for His!"

SCENE XI

"My Life for His!"

166   Returned Empty

wet Lady, her wedding ring, on his thrown
finger.

She marked the strong, quick strokes.
Rapidly he put distance between himself
and the shore. She had to keep adjusting
the focus.

Then she prayed—or so it seemed to him—
. . . .

He had not told her
. . . .

bore in the sunshine on the . . . .

Scene XI

"MY LIFE FOR HIS!"

WHEN Lady Tintagel stepped out on to the balcony and took her stand beside the telescope, a deathly sense of faintness almost overcame her. She gripped the balustrade to keep herself from falling.

Gradually she revived in the fresh morning air.

Then she adjusted the telescope and focused it on the dark head in the water.

The powerful lens brought the swimmer so near, that it seemed as if she had but to put out her hand to touch him.

He was swimming in direct line between herself and the rising sun. The water through which he moved, sparkled and glittered. She could see every strand of his wet hair, her wedding-ring on his brown finger.

She marked the strong, quick strokes. Rapidly he put distance between himself and the shore. She had to keep adjusting the focus to hold him near.

" Oh God," she prayed, " do not let him do this thing. Do not let him drown. If a life must be given, my life for his. Oh, by the mercy of Christ, my life for his ! "

She saw the wild birds swoop above him.

After a while he began to flag. She watched him fold his arms, turn upon his back, and lie, like a tired child, upon the bosom of the sparkling ocean.

Then she could see his face, ghastly in the sunlight. There was madness in it— madness.

" Oh God of infinite mercy ! My punishment is greater than I can bear. I' bow to Thy Divine Will. I give up my belovèd ; I give him up, if need be, for all eternity ; but save him from the doom of suicide. My life for his, O Lord, my life for his ! "

He had turned, and was swimming on; but his movements were vague and uncertain. He clove the water feebly, pausing between each stroke and raising his head.

Suddenly he disappeared. The sparkling highway held no sign of him.

"Nigel!" she shrieked, "Nigel!"

The brown hands reappeared; the dark head rose out of the sea. But making no attempt to swim, he lifted his face to the sun, then raised his arms and went down again.

"O God, have mercy!"

Oh, mocking, vast expanse of gaily sparkling sea!

She held her breath and watched.

Ah! His hands again! His face—the eyes now wide and staring. He gasped; his chest heaved. He raised his head and shoulders out of the water; then slowly clasped his hands, lifted them above his head, and sank instantly.

She was silent in her agony; yet, speechless, her heart still cried to God.

"Save him! Save him! My soul for his! O God, my soul for his!"

O empty, sunlit sea.

The floor rocked and swayed beneath her feet. She clung to the telescope, striving to keep in view the rippling surface where last she had seen him.

No sign, no hope. This was the end.

An awful calmness held her. "Fifty fathoms deep," and this time no return. She and Despair must company together through all the years to come and after.

No! O God, his hands! And now his head, his heaving, gasping chest!

He fought and struck the water, then straightened out and lay upon his back, heaving, breathing; breathing, heaving; gasping with closed eyes; then quite still, resting; a weary child upon its mother's breast; a lover in the tender arms of his belovèd. The water rocked him gently. So near he seemed. She clung to the telescope, speaking softly to him.

"Nigel, my dearest, God has heard my

prayer. Rest there, dear Heart. The arms of Eternal Love are beneath you. Oh, if the wish to live returns, you will be given strength to reach the shore. Heart of my heart, my life for yours ; my *soul* for yours, if need be."

His eyes were open. He was gazing skyward. A look of ineffable joy and peace was on his face.

" Oh, what does he see ? Visions of God ? Promise of life and peace and joy restored ? Or is he dying ; dying there, before my eyes ? Nigel, my own, what is it ? "

Slowly he turned and looked toward the shore ; then started swimming, a steady breast-stroke, slow but sure.

Her trembling fingers adjusted the focus, keeping pace with him.

His eyes met hers. A glory of love was on his face. He waved his arm and smiled. His lips moved and formed a word.

Yes, it was her name !

" Miriam," he said ; and again, " Miriam!"

" Oh, wonder beyond belief. He has

remembered and is coming back to me; coming back a second time from the dead; but this time God-sent, God-given."

She laughed softly and whispered tender words.

"Yes, darling, I know. Yes, your wife is here; just waiting here, as on those dear mornings long ago. . . . Swim carefully, my dearest boy. I do so dread the sea—so deep and treacherous. . . . Yes, I see the ring. . . . Oh, is that how you love me? No, don't stop to answer. . . . Nigel, it takes so long. . . . Are you exhausted, darling? Oh, turn again and rest. . . . Nigel, you make no progress. Oh, my God, he is swimming, but he is not moving! He is caught by the current! . . . Ah! . . . No! . . . Yes! He is gone!"

She flew into her room and pealed the bell. Then back to the balcony, shrieking wildly. So near the shore, but gone.

An empty sea; a cruel, sparkling, empty sea!

The sound of hurrying feet within. She

staggered back into the room, clutching at the window-frame and curtains.

"Quick, Thomas, quick! Sir Nigel—drowning—below the cliff—a boat—a rope——"

Then she fell forward on her face.

SCENE XII

The Deep Well

Scene XII

THE DEEP WELL

WHEN Luke Sparrow awoke from
a long sleep, he found himself
in bed, wrapped in softest blankets,
in the room to which he had been taken on
the previous evening.

His entire being was permeated by that
extraordinary sense of comfort which
accompanies returning strength after violent
exertion. He had no desire to move, yet he
lifted his right arm and looked with a
perplexed smile at the sleeve of a blue silk
sleeping suit. Then he saw the wedding-
ring upon his finger.

" Miriam ! "

He let a flood of tender memory sweep
over him.

" Miriam ! My wife."

Presently he looked round the room,

taking in every detail. It was familiar in a strange, double way. His conscious brain remembered each impression of the night before, when he thought it "Colin's" dressing-room; but a vague, dream-like memory, working slowly, like drawing water from the depths of a deep well, remembered it as his own.

He studied the engravings on the walls, seeing them consciously for the first time; but when he looked away, it seemed to him that he had known, before looking, that each would be in its place.

He looked along the row of books in the bookcase. His conscious mind mastered their titles; but from the deep well of his sub-consciousness he drew the knowledge of what, if he could open them, he would find written on the fly-leaves.

This experiment soon tired him. He lifted his hand again and fixed his mind upon the wedding-ring, and upon her whose ring it was.

Nothing vague here, nothing indefinite.

His love for her, his memory of her love, flowed through him like new wine. Her loveliness, her tenderness, her sweet fidelity.

He held the ring against his lips. "My bride"—what memories! "My wife, my perfect mate!"

To him, who had never loved, it came as an overwhelming wonder to find himself in sudden possession of a love full grown.

"Miriam! Miriam!"

Soon he would see her. She was somewhere quite near.

Oh, heart of gold, beating beneath the garment of soft woman's flesh!

He closed his eyes and gave himself up to the exquisite enchantment. The purity of each remembrance of her love and his, filled him with a sense of heavenly rapture.

"My perfect one; my Angel of Delight!"

The door opened softly. An elderly woman appeared, stout and matronly, carrying a cup on a small tray. She advanced to the side of the bed.

He had never seen her before. He studied the kind, homely face, the neat black gown, the silk apron, the cairngorm brooch. Then from the depths of the well came up an intuition and, almost before he knew it, he had said: "Hullo, Mary."

The ruddy face paled. The hand holding the tray shook.

"Yes, Sir Nigel. We thought you might have wakened, Sir Nigel. I have made bold to bring you broth."

Broth? Yes, of course. Broth and Mary would go together. He sat up, took it from her hand, and supped it hungrily.

She watched him, with eyes which held a strange mingling of love, fear, and wonder. The love, a life-long fidelity. The fear came with the remembrance of a coffin beside which she had stood; of a grave in the churchyard on the hill side. The wonder was born of a mystery, unexplained, unaccountable, but accepted with the simple faith of a mind ruled by the heart.

" How did I get here, Mary ? "

" Thomas will tell you, Sir Nigel."

" You tell me. I like hearing your dear old voice."

" Thomas found you by the rocks, Sir Nigel. He fetched the foresters, and they brought you up on a hurdle."

" How did Thomas know I had been swimming ? "

" Her ladyship gave the alarm."

" Ah ! Who put me to bed ? "

" Thomas and the doctor."

" The doctor ! What doctor ? "

" They fetched the doctor, Sir Nigel."

" I see. Thank you, Mary ; the broth was very good. Now, where are my clothes ? I want to get up."

" I will send Thomas, Sir Nigel."

Left alone, he pondered. What had they told this doctor ? Would he also rise, a familiar figure, from the well of subconscious memory ?

The door opened again. The old butler entered, closing it carefully behind him.

"Thomas, come here. I have been talking to Mary."

"So I hear, Sir Nigel."

"She tells me the foresters carried me up from the shore. Do they know me, Thomas ? "

"No, Sir Nigel. They are young men, sons of Fergusson and Graem."

"I see. How about this doctor ? "

"He has been her ladyship's medical attendant for a matter of twenty-five years, Sir Nigel."

"Twenty-five years ? Ah ! What did you say to him ? How did you explain my presence here ? "

"We told him you were an old friend of her ladyship's whom she had met abroad."

"Abroad ? " He dived into the well. "Ah yes ! That was true, wasn't it. Where——"

"Italy, Sir Nigel."

"Yes ; Florence. Good Lord ! What else did you tell the doctor ? "

"That you dined here last evening, and spent the night; went for an early swim this morning, and got caught by the current."

"Good. Who else—er—remembers, beside you and Mary?"

"No one, Sir Nigel. We alone are left, of the old staff."

"Thomas, bring my clothes. I must get up."

"See the doctor first, Sir Nigel."

"No need. I am all right. There is but one person I want to see. Where is she, Thomas?"

"Her ladyship is in her room, Sir Nigel." The old man's face worked. "The doctor is with her ladyship."

"The doctor? What's up, Thomas? Is anything wrong?"

"Wrong? Wrong, Sir Nigel? Merciful God!" He wrung his hands helplessly. "It's best you should hear it from me, Sir Nigel. Our dear lady is dying. We thought she was gone when we found her. But the doctor brought remedies in his bag. He revived her. She is conscious again, and knows us. But he says she can't last through the day."

He leapt from the bed.

" Quick ! My clothes."

" For God's sake, sir, be calm ! For her ladyship's sake ; for all our sakes. It will seem like madness. Don't do aught that might disturb her peace. The country side will ring with it. They have talked for years. They will say she died insane."

" My clothes, Thomas."

" Those you came in are soaked with sea water, Sir Nigel. But we have plenty here. Her ladyship had them all kept ready, and always brushed and aired."

He went to a chest of drawers and fumbled blindly

" Your flannels, Sir Nigel ? She would like best to see you in what you wore that day. The coat you flung to her as you ran down the beach, she keeps in her own room. But here are all the others complete."

With trembling hands, he laid them on a chair. "All you need is here, Sir Nigel."

"Then leave me, Thomas. But come back in five minutes."

He dressed rapidly.

"Dying! My wife dying! She shall not die. By heaven, she shall not die!"

As he slipped on the coat, there came a quick rap on the door.

"Yes; come in! Now, Thomas——" Ah, the doctor. With an effort he pulled himself together. "Good morning."

"So you're up and dressed? I thought you would soon be all right when that stupor of exhaustion passed into natural sleep. You'll do. I did what I could for you, Mr.——"

"My name is Luke Sparrow."

"Ah, Mr. Sparrow. But my hands were full, from the first, with poor Lady Tintagel. Sad business, very. And the daughter and son-in-law went off motoring early this morning a four days' tour, leaving no address. Haven't traced them yet. Stupid thing to do. Not that she wants them, poor lady. And the quieter she is, the better. But she is asking for you."

The little man jerked over to the window, and fussed with the blind cord.

" Is there any immediate danger ? "

" Danger ?   My dear sir, she is dying, would have been dead now, had I not had powerful restoratives handy. She can't last out the day. Her heart has been dicky for years. Any shock might have done this. Thirty years ago her husband was drowned before her eyes—as you may have heard—down on this beach. A most devoted couple, so I'm told. Wrapped up, etc. ; you know the sort of thing. The shock nearly killed her. Look at that wonderful white hair ! It isn't age. It was as white as it is to-day, when they went to her the morning after he was drowned, and she only twenty-eight, and beautiful as a June morning. I came to these parts a couple of years later. Sad case ! She recovered physically, bar the heart trouble !

but her mind has been touched on one point ever since. Always expecting him back. Sea give up its dead, I suppose. You know the kind of thing? I always say they should have let her see the corpse; might have cured her. But, after a week in the water! Not a pretty sight, you know. Acted for the best no doubt. Oh, she never speaks of it to me. But people talk you know; say she always keeps his room ready, and so forth. Mania, of course, but harmless, poor lady. Why do fine chaps such as he, throw away their lives for worthless young women; couldn't sail a boat; better drowned. Thousand pities. So she watches the sea and, I suppose, saw you in difficulties. Gave her a shock; brought back the scene. Thomas and his wife are very close; told me nothing. But her maid—nice girl —said she shrieked: 'Sir Nigel is drowning below the cliff; a boat! a rope!' Poor soul! Sane enough, now; but heart done for."

"May I see her?"

" Why not ?   She keeps asking for you, so Mrs. Thomas tells me.   She will be gone at once, if she makes any effort or sits up. But she can't last out the day, and she may as well have what she wants and die happy, as die, three hours later, wanting it.   I had a patient once who was dying ; apparently nothing could save her ; and she wanted to go out into her garden, lovely garden it was, too.   Nurses and relations wouldn't hear of it.   ' Why, doctor, it might kill her ! '   ' Good Lord,' said I, ' and if it does ? Let her die in the garden, if she wishes. Isn't it a sweeter place to die in than her bed ? '   So they carried her out, and blest if she didn't rally from that hour and get well !   Queer things, bodies !   Well, I must be off.   There's nothing further to be done here ; and I've a baby on hand, waiting to enter the world, which is, after all, of more importance than a lady waiting to make her exit."

" Can nothing be done to relieve——"

" She is in no pain, and won't be.   I will

be back in three hours. You will stay on,
I suppose, and being an old friend, you can
see to things, until these motorists are
found. A shock for them, but they deserve
it ; going off and leaving no address ! And
between ourselves, they'll be pleased to
come into the property and the money.
They've not been much to her, nor she to
them. She was what I called ' *a one man*
woman.' While she had him, because he
filled her heart, it was open to all. But
when she lost him, she lost her all, and
her empty heart closed to others. That is
why I curse those French girls ; throttling
that splendid fellow with their foolish fingers.
Who wanted them ? And at such a cost !
Well, good-bye, for the present——"

"Can you not leave instructions as to
what is to be done for Lady Tintagel ? "

"The housekeeper has full instructions,
and I have left stimulating draughts with
her. Keep the patient quiet. Give her all
she wants. Do, without question, everything she asks. Don't let more than one

person be in her room at the same time, unless help is needed. Don't attempt to move her. She lies where they put her at first, on a couch near the window, looking out over the sea. I wouldn't let them move her. It's such a silly fad always to want people to die in their beds. It rejoices my heart when I hear of a parson dying in the pulpit. Please God, I'll either die in my gig or on the links. Good morning, Mr. Sparrow. See you later on."

Silence at last.

He went over to the window, and leaned his forehead against the glass.

He must go to her now. She wanted him, and time was short. Thank God, he would have her alone. Surely Divine interposition had given them thus to each other. He must just wait until he could be sure that the noisy little man, who had filled the room with babel, was clear out of the house.

Mrs. Thomas tapped and entered.

"Her ladyship asks for you, Sir Nigel. She is alone."

"Shew me to her room, Mary," he said; but in the same moment, turning from her, walked across the room, drew back a curtain and found the door of communication behind it. He opened it. Double doors. Yes, of course. She had liked the absolute security of double doors to their own room.

One moment he waited, took a deep breath, laid firm hold upon himself; then opened the door, and passed into the quiet room beyond.

"Her ladyship asks for you, Sir Nigel. She is alone."

"Show me to her room, Mary," he said; but in the same moment, turning from her, walked across the room, drew back a curtain and found the door of communication behind it. He opened it. Double doors. Yes, of course. She had liked the absolute security of double doors to their own room.

One moment he waited, took a deep breath, laid firm hold upon himself; then opened the door, and passed into the quiet room beyond.

SCENE XIII

"Nevertheless——"

Scene XIII

"NEVERTHELESS——"

SHE lay upon the couch, near the open window, very white and still.

She was gazing out across the sea but, as he closed the door, she turned her eyes and watched him, while he walked over to the couch; and those patient eyes were so full of unutterable love and longing, that his throat closed on the words he had meant to say.

He knelt down beside her, took both her hands in his, and laid his lips upon them.

"Miriam! Miriam!"

"Nigel, you do remember?"

"Yes, my belovèd, my wife, my own— thank God, I do remember. And I love you with every fibre of my being."

He knew the time was short. There must be no delay.

He drew her wedding-ring from his finger, slipped it back to its rightful place, and laid his lips on ring and finger together.

" I love you utterly," he said, " and I hold you mine for ever."

" Nigel, my husband, this time it is I who go, and you who remain behind. You will be braver than I."

" My own," he answered, " we shall be together in the place where alone true joys are to be found ; safe within the circle of the Will of God. Since I left you and went out into the sunrise, I, who before was empty, have become rich beyond all human comprehension in the possession of three different memories. I remember the thirty years of this present life. I remember the precious love which was ours in the life before, and, remembering that, my heart has grown so rich that I care not to re-member aught else of that life, but just the utter sweetness of our wedded love. And,

best of all, it has been granted me to
remember something of the wonder of that
eternal Dwelling Place—that short while in
Eternity, before our great love drew me
back to Time—not in detail, but in its
larger lines of truth."

"Ah, tell me that," she whispered. "I
know the precious past. I know much
of the present. Tell me of the Eternity
between."

"God's love," he said, "is the great
Dwelling Place; God's Will, the very air
we breathe. The passionate desire of every
soul, freed from the earthly prison of the
flesh is to return that love, to do that Will.
The Son of God, walking the earth as man
—though emptied, for the time being, of
His eternal memory—remembered this, and
gave His fellow-men the perfect prayer :
'Thy will be done in earth, as it is in
Heaven.' When that prayer finds its complete fulfilment, earth's hard perplexities
will all be solved, earth's tears all wiped
away. His perfect Will ensures man's

perfect joy. The next petition in the pattern prayer bears out this thought. 'Give us this day our daily bread.' What food is to the body, doing the Will of God is to the soul. He Who taught us thus to pray, was the one man who could say with absolute honesty: 'My meat is to do the Will of Him that sent me.'

"All souls know this by instinct. The sinner knows it in his sin, and fails to find in sin a lasting pleasure. The agnostic knows it in his search after something which can meet and satisfy the craving of his mind. The martyr knows it, and laughs at the cruel flame. The angels know it, and fly swiftly on strong wings. Christ knew it, in Gethsemane, and hushed the natural protest of His human agony, and summed up His life's purpose in those perfect words: 'Nevertheless, not my will, but Thine be done.' When the last rebel soul has yielded and understood, then the great End will come; God will be All in all."

He paused and laid his forehead upon her folded hands.

" My wife, our sacred love must stand this test. This is the fire which burns up all the dross, but leaves us, as eternal treasure the gold and precious stones.

" Just now I woke, filled with the rapture of our love, the joy, beyond all words, of having found you. Almost at once, I heard that I must lose you. My flesh cried out : ' I cannot let her go !' Then came the Angel of His love and pity, and laid a strengthening hand upon my soul, and said : ' This is God's will, His perfect way for her and you.' Belovèd, to that Will we both must bow. Thus shall we find our purest joy, and love which has no ending."

" Nigel," she whispered, " I brought you back empty, and I leave you desolate."

He waited till his voice was steady, then replied :

" Listen, sweet wife of mine ! Our love has brought me Home. Through you there comes to me this chance to put myself once

more within the Will of God. Together we
accept in faith and patience, this parting
we are called upon to face, and thus atone
for the mistaken past. Mine is the harder
part, I know ; but I would have it so. I
left you to the harder part before. I shall
be lonely, but not desolate. I owe a debt to
life for thirty selfish, wasted years. If a
great chance comes, I may pay it soon.
That will be as God wills. But, be the parting long or short, always I shall know you
watch and wait for me ; and, thanks again
to you, I shall not be earth-bound ; for,
where my Treasure is, there will my heart
be also."

At last he lifted his head and looked at
her.

Then his courage almost broke. That
lovely face, so dear, so well-remembered.
Those lips, parting in soft surrender. The
tenderness his heart so hungered for, dwelling upon him in those dying eyes.

"Oh, I can't," he said, and hid his face
against her breast. "My God, give us one

year ! If it be possible, let this cup pass."

She laid her hands upon his head and held him close.

" ' Nevertheless——' " she said : " Oh, Nigel, finish it ! "

And, in a voice broken by sobs, he spoke the sacred words which make complete a brave soul's sacrifice.

SCENE XIV

"No Sadness of Farewell"

Scene XIV

"NO SADNESS OF FAREWELL"

THE hours which followed seemed to him the nearest approach to heaven a man could know on earth.

Sometimes she lay in his arms and gently slept; then roused herself to drink what Mary brought, and rallying a little, let her eyes dwell on his face, as he sat beside her in the sunshine, talking softly of many things—the past, the future; all their love had meant; would mean.

Deep peace enveloped them. Time stood still and waited while they drank deeply of a fount of love, slaking the thirst of years. Words could scarce carry the tender emotion of all they had to say to one another. Because of her great weakness, it was chiefly he who spoke and she who listened. But sometimes she rallied, and uttered words which he knew he would carry in his heart for ever.

Twice he left her; when the doctor returned amazed to find her still alive, and so content; and when she sent for Thomas, to bid the faithful old man farewell, and to give him last instructions.

This time, when Luke returned, she beckoned to him anxiously.

"Nigel, all this is yours; the house, the property; all should be yours."

He smiled. "My dearest, no! Not this time. *You* are mine, and I want nothing more. I arrived with a knapsack; I shall depart with a knapsack. I am just a tramp, you know; but a happy tramp, with a kingdom in my heart."

"Nigel—one thing—you will not refuse? My despatch-box—full of letters—yours and mine; and the photographs. You will take that?"

"Yes, my belovèd, I gladly will."

"A few other things are in it—sacred to

us; a miniature you had done of me the year before—you went. And lately—I have kept—in a sealed envelope—a thousand pounds in bank notes, in case of just such an emergency as this. Nigel—you will? To please me? It is all yours, really. You might wish to go abroad—travel——"

He hesitated. "Miriam, I have all I need." Her eyes pleaded. "All right, my darling. The case and all that's in it. Your gift to me." He bent and kissed her fluttering fingers. "Don't be troubled, dear Heart. Such a perfect thought of yours. I will do beautiful things with it; things you would have liked to plan. They will be my own wife's gifts to me."

She smiled and closed her eyes, content.

At sunset he knew their one day was over.

He gave her the draught the doctor had left for a last emergency, and momentarily she revived.

Her eyes left his face, to gaze across the sea.

"'Sunset and evening star,'" she whispered, "'And one clear call for me.' Say it, Nigel."

His great love made him brave.

He repeated the lines, and the deep, sweet music of his voice, as it reached her, held no tremor. Only, he looked away across the sea ; not at the dying face.

"'No sadness of farewell,'" she said. "Nigel, is that possible ? "

Then he turned, smiling bravely.

"All is possible, my dearest, to a perfect love."

"Oh, raise me," she whispered, " and take me in your arms."

He held her close.

She lifted her face to his.

That look of love unspeakable, broke his iron self-control.

His tears fell on her face.

"I know ! " she said, and suddenly her voice was strong and full. " My lover and my husband ! But it is all joy—no sadness really. And such a little while——"

" All joy, my wife," he answered ; then, bending, laid his lips on hers.

And in that perfect kiss, her spirit passed.

SCENE XV

"The Secrets of Our Hearts"

Scene XV

"THE SECRETS OF OUR HEARTS"

THE stranger from the inn stood with the mourners at the open grave, in the churchyard on the hillside.

The son and daughter glanced across, and wondered vaguely who he was, and why he stood so near.

Another coffin, hidden during thirty years, had seen the light that day; for the bricked grave had been so planned that two might lie within it, side by side.

Into the empty space they lowered the new coffin, with its bright silver fittings and polished wood, slipping it carefully into place beside the one which had rested there so long.

The mourners bent and looked into the grave, while the new coffin slowly passed

from view; but the stranger kept his eyes
lifted to the tree tops. His quiet face, so
striking in its dark beauty, shewed no signs
of deep emotion; yet, to many there, he
seemed to be chief mourner.

Man that is born of a woman hath but a
short time to live, and is full of misery. He
cometh up, and is cut down, like a flower;
he fleeth as it were a shadow, and never
continueth in one stay.

In the midst of life we are in death: of
whom may we seek for succour, but of Thee,
O Lord, Who for our sins art justly
displeased?

Yet, O Lord God most holy, O Lord
most mighty, O holy and most merciful
Saviour, deliver us not into the bitter pains
of eternal death.

Thou knowest, Lord, the secrets of our
hearts; shut not Thy merciful ears to our
prayer; but spare us, Lord most holy, O
God most mighty, O holy and merciful
Saviour, Thou most worthy Judge eternal,
suffer us not, at our last hour, for any pains
of death, to fall from Thee.

As the handful of earth fell with a
sudden thud upon the coffin, the stranger
started, seemed to awake to the actualities

around him, took a step forward, and looked down into the grave.

Yes ; side by side they lay—the two. One looked very grand and new beside the other, though careful hands had polished that and made it passable, to face the light of day.

The inscription on the large brass plate was clearly legible, and left no doubt as to what lay beneath the lid.

NIGEL GUIDO CARDROSS TINTAGEL

Aged 30

Drowned August 12th, 1883

Greater love hath no man than this : that a man lay down his life for his friends.

While he pondered these words, in solemn awe and silence, there fell upon his ears the Church's triumphant promise of Life, which overcomes the grave ; of faith, which changes death to life eternal.

𝕺 merciful God, the Father of our Lord Jesus Christ, Who is the resurrection and the life ; in 𝔚hom whosoever believeth shall live, though he die ; and whosoever liveth, and believeth in Him, shall not die eternally. . . . 𝔚e meekly beseech Thee, O Father, to raise us from the death of sin unto the life of righteousness ; that, when we shall depart this life, we may rest in Him, as our hope is this our sister doth——

" This our sister ? "   The shadow of a smile passed across the dark face, gazing so intently at the two coffins. How well he knew that the one, whatever its brass plate might say, held only a suit of clothes, spoilt by sea water, empty and done with. How easy it made it for him to realise that this new coffin, inscribed

MIRIAM TINTAGEL

also held naught save an empty gown—a very lovely robe, sacred and precious, because worn by her, but nothing more.

" Miriam, belovèd ! Do you smile to see us standing here in our trappings of woe ? Can you look back through that open door by which you passed into the radiance of

Eternity, and see this little patch of Time, and mark the pomp and ceremony with which your worn-out garment is laid to rest beside mine ? Do you see your husband, as he stands looking down upon his own coffin ? And do you understand how strange is the experience, one through which probably no other man has ever passed ? "

The grace of our Lord Jesus Christ, and the love of God, and the fellowship of the Holy Ghost, be with us all evermore. *Amen.*

It was over at last, that tenderest of all the sacred services in the great Church's Liturgy. Living and Dead were alike dismissed with those comprehensive words of grace, love, and fellowship; the threefold blessing of the Triune God.

SCENE XVI

"Who Was He?"

Scene XVI

"WHO WAS HE?"

COLIN and Eva walked down the hill together, sympathetic friends and humble dependents standing aside to let them pass.

They talked in low voices, decorously; but the sense of relief from tension which follows on a funeral, shewed in their brightening faces, as they turned with undisguised pleasure toward the beautiful house which was now their own possession.

"Colin, I know why that man's face seemed familiar to me. You remember I whispered to you when we noticed him in the church that I was certain I had seen him before?"

"Well? Had you?"

"No. But—it's very curious. Just as we turned from the grave—you saw how he stood gazing down at the coffins ?—he looked up, and his eyes met mine. Then I remembered. He is extraordinarily like the photographs of my father."

" Could he be a relation ? "

" Not that I know of. My father was an only child, and I never heard of cousins."

" Well, we can tell Thomas to find out who he is. I say, dear ! Won't tea be nice ! Let's have it in the Oak Room. I shall make that my smoking-room, if you have no objection."

SCENE XVII
In the Pine Wood

Scene XVII

IN THE PINE WOOD

LUKE SPARROW strode through the pine woods, taking a short cut from the churchyard back to the inn.

His train for the south left in an hour.

Hurrying footsteps came behind him. At first he took them for an echo of his own; then realised that he was being followed, and walked the faster. He had no wish to be accosted.

"Sir Nigel! Sir Nigel!"

He stopped and turned sharply.

Old Thomas, breathless, in deepest black, was hastening down the stony path.

"Your pardon, Sir Nigel. May I speak with you?"

"What is it, old friend?"

"Sir Nigel, you are going? Don't leave

us behind, Mary and me. Now we have
lost our dear lady, we cannot stay here. Already there are changes. We shall not be
wanted. We know too much about our
lady's ways and wishes. Pipes in the Oak
Room she never did allow, nor whisky and
soda in the morning. Her ladyship's last
word to me was : ' If possible, go with Sir
Nigel, Thomas, you and Mary. You know
his ways, and I would like to feel Mary
was there to do his mending and airing,
and see that he has properly cooked meals.'
Our dear lady has left an annuity of two
hundred a year between us, and we
have our savings, and no encumbrances,
thank God. It isn't a question of wages ;
it's a question of home, and the Fam'ly
—boy and man, Sir Nigel, for over fifty
years."

  He paused for breath and a pocket-hand-
kerchief.

  " Your pardon, Sir Nigel." He wiped the
tears from his furrowed cheeks. " Boy and
man, Sir Nigel, for half a century. I ran

beside your pony, sir, as you may remember."

"I don't remember, Thomas; but *She* did; and I have no doubt you do."

He considered.

Was it really Her wish?

He thought of the thousand pounds in bank notes in the despatch-box at the inn.

"Of course you shall come, old friend; and Mary with you. But I have no home as yet. We must make one together. I am going south by the express. Could you be happy in London? I will find a cosy flat. As soon as I have found it, I will send for you and Mary."

The old man blew his nose.

"Beg pardon, Sir Nigel." His relief was pathetic. "We felt if we lost you again, we lost all. It isn't a matter of money. It's service, and our lady's wishes, and love of you, Sir Nigel. Boy and man——"

"Right. Tell Mary the thing's settled, I'm off in an hour, Thomas. I don't want any awkward questions."

H

" True, Sir Nigel. The doctor wanted to
know why you had left the house before the
new master and mistress arrived. He had
counted on you to give them full particulars
of our lady's last hours. He has been hin-
dered from coming over until to-day, by a
very serious case. As I say to Mary, there
are always dispensations ! But he has gone
down to the house now. And you were
noticed at the grave. There will be talk
in every home by nightfall. Douglas saw
you, and Fergusson and old Nannie Steer.
You remember them, Sir Nigel ? "

No. The sub-conscious well was rapidly
growing deeper, its memories more elusive.
Douglas, Fergusson, old Nannie Steer, con-
veyed nothing to him. Only his Treasure
in the heavens was inalienably his own.
But he began to realise how largely his sub-
consciousness had drawn from hers. With
her departure from this earthly setting, all
its memories were fading into dream-like
vagueness.

" To see you standing at the grave, Sir

Nigel, looking down at *that* coffin! It was like the Judgment Day. It made my blood run cold; and Mary well-nigh swooned."

"It need not have, Thomas; any more than when I stood looking down into that drawer when you shewed me my old suits, folded, and laid away by careful hands."

He stood, looking upwards. A shaft of sunlight, piercing through the pines, fell on his face.

"Neither my wife nor I are in that grave. There is no death, old friend. That which we call death is fuller life—life more abundant."

"Speaking of clothes, Sir Nigel, and such like, her ladyship gave me orders to pack everything in the dressing-room in two trunks and keep them in our quarters until I knew where to send them. Her ladyship wished you to have the things she had so treasured. None ever went into that room, save her ladyship and myself; or Mary, if our lady was away. So no questions will be asked when they find it bare. Her ladyship also gave me a list of furniture she has left to me and Mary, meaning it for you; her couch in the Oak Room, your pipe-rack, her writing-table, her easy chair, and a few other things. She dictated the paper and signed it that morning while the doctor was with her; but she told me, by word of mouth, they were left to us, for you."

So this was her way of making sure that he should have a home, filled with sweet memories of her. Oh, Miriam, belovèd! Now it was for him to find that home, for himself and these two faithful souls.

"Very well, Thomas. They can come with you and Mary when the home is ready. I will try for a jolly little house, not a flat. It will be more home-like. Whatever she wished, or said, or did, is right. Only be careful no questions are asked. You know what people would say if they knew of the happenings of this past week? They would say that she, and you, and I, were mad."

The old man smiled. "It don't matter what folk say, Sir Nigel. All that really

matters, is what our own hearts know;
and that her ladyship died happy."

As Luke Sparrow walked on alone, at a
rapid pace, through the pine woods, he
repeated those words to himself. "All that
really matters is what our own hearts
know." Aye, how true! That, and one
thing more. "Thou knowest, Lord, the
secrets of our hearts."

SCENE XVIII

The Home She Planned

Scene XVIII

THE HOME SHE PLANNED

Three months later

L UKE SPARROW sat at his writing-table reading " proof."

The cosy study was filled with books and littered with the work he loved.

Presently, with noiseless step, entered old Thomas; turned on the lights, made the fire blaze, stealthily tidied the room, moved a small table to the couch, and brought in the tea.

" Take it while it's hot, Sir Nigel."

" All right, Thomas."

" Mary has made a dish of those bannocks, Sir Nigel, of which you and her ladyship used to be so fond."

" Mary is a wonder, Thomas. Her memory is as excellent as her cooking. All

233

right; I'll take half an hour off. I've done a good day's work already. . . . No; don't draw the curtains yet awhile. There may be some lonely soul passing by, in the cold and dark out there, who will enjoy the sight of this cosy warmth and brightness. I will draw them, when I get back to work."

As the old man left the room, closing the door behind him, Luke Sparrow pushed aside his mass of papers, rose, flung himself upon the couch, stretched his limbs, and shook off the strain of long hours of concentration.

A tempting tea tray, arranged with much care and thought, was at his elbow. Mary's golden bannocks stood for memories—memories not his own; but he took them, on trust, from Mary.

The room was a perfect combination of work and comfort; outside interests and home.

He took a miniature-case from his pocket and opened it. Exquisitely painted on ivory, the lovely face looked out at him ; the lips smiled their message of abiding tenderness. It had been painted before the night which turned that bright hair white. Of all the treasures he had found in the despatch-box, this meant the most to him.

He looked long at it now, as he sat alone upon that couch on which he had once lain with her arms wrapped around him.

"Miriam, belovèd," he said, "I think you would like this home of ours. And I believe you would like my book. And I am sure you would be amused to know that Mary drags old Thomas out 'of an evening' to see 'the pictures.' Mary is having the time of her life, and Thomas thinks it is bad for Mary's soul. But you and I would agree that Mary's soul can stand a little more gaiety than her life with Thomas has hitherto provided.

"Now I must pour out my own tea from your beautiful William the Fourth silver teapot, so solid and embossed, and sturdy

on its little feet, with a pair of acorns on
the lid.

"Miriam, do you know how lonely it is
to have all this, yet not to have you? And
so slowly the months pass; and so many
years are yet to come.

"Oh, my belovèd! Send me thoughts of
hope and patience, and strength to play the
man."

SCENE XIX
The Great Chance

Scene XIX

THE GREAT CHANCE

Ten months later

LUKE SPARROW, erect and vigorous, in the khaki uniform which had begun to mean so much to England, stood on his study hearth-rug, giving final instructions to his old servant.

"I'm in luck, Thomas. So early in the day; but I lost no time, and it's France for me to-morrow; and, please God, that means Belgium, and in the thick of it. You will look after things, till I get back. Don't let Mary fret. Give her a cheerful time.

"If I don't return, my things will come back to you. My will is in that drawer. Everything will belong to you two faithful souls. That is what her ladyship would wish. . . . That's all right, Thomas. Yes, I know all about it.   Good-bye, old friend. . . .

"And now send Mary to me. I must have one dear woman to hug me good-bye before I go."

SCENE XX

"Coming !"

Scene XX

" COMING ! "

Four years later

A FOREST of white crosses on the battlefields of France.

Two British soldiers moved among them, seeking a special name.

At length they found it.

Luke Sparrow

" Ah, here it is ! Here he lies. Well, there are many above ground, hale and hearty, who but for him would be lying as he lies to-day ; and I'm one of them.

" Brave ? Good Lord, he didn't know what fear meant ! Each time he went over the top you might have thought he was going to his bridal. He used to call this bloody war the Great Chance. And such a pal! Do you mind how it kept our spirits up only to look at him, let alone his hand on your shoulder or his voice in your ear?

"But life-saving was his passion. No place was too hot for him, if a helpless man lay there to be brought in. V.C.? He earned it thirty times over! And always came through all right.

"But at last they got him, and no mistake about it. Both legs, and through the chest; past operating.

"I was with him at the end. He'd been lying very still, just groaning a bit on the quiet; when suddenly he rises up on his elbow and shouts, 'Coming!' clear as a bugle call. 'Coming!' he says, and falls back dead."

The two stood looking at the simple white cross and the grave it marked; then turned to watch an old man, in sombre clothing, who moved among the graves, anxiously seeking. He carried in his hand a wreath of immortelles.

At last he drew near, read Luke Sparrow's

name, and, baring his head, fell upon his knees beside the cross, and sobbed.

The soldiers turned away, respecting the old man's grief.

After a while he rose, laid the wreath at the foot of the cross, and went his way.

Luke Sparrow's comrades came back and stooped to read what was written on a card attached to the wreath.

" Hullo ! " said one, " The old chap has made a mistake. See here ! "

To

SIR NIGEL GUIDO CARDROSS TINTAGEL, BART.

in faithful and loving remembrance
from his humble servants
Mary and Thomas

*Greater love hath no man than this : that a
man lay down his life for his friends.*

" Leave it alone," said the other soldier. " He was worth a score of barts ! Let him keep the wreath."

Then they also went their way.

And the winds of God blew gently over that forest of plain crosses, bearing the vast army of heroic names, which are not forgotten before God, but inscribed for ever in the Book of Life.

"O years! And Age! Farewell:
   Behold I go,
   Where I do know
Infinity to dwell.

 And these mine eyes shall see
   All times, how they
   Are lost i' the Sea
Of vast Eternity.

Where never Moon shall sway
   The Stars ; but she
   And Night, shall be
Drown'd in one endless Day."

ROBERT HERRICK (1629).